MLAMLELI REDEEMER

FEMINISM OF LILITH

WOMAN'S STRIFE FOR INDEPENDENCE

Contents

1

Adam and Lilith's relationship breaks apart

Who could have guessed that humankind was formed and that humans emerged from the dust of the earth? The man who had materialized could tell of his priceless finding of life and the birth of a son, Adam, and a daughter, Lilith.

To aspire to be like him as a creator, he endowed mankind with his likeness, intelligence, power, and ability to recreate. It's not clear to me that he thought Adam and Lilith would be created in his likeness, albeit with distinct personalities. He bestowed power and sovereignty upon Adam over every kingdoms and persons in the realm of Midgard. This is the planet Earth.

Lilith was bestowed with the ability to assist and encourage Adam in adorning his realm. He crowned them with his splendor and set them eastward of the Elysian Plain in order to preserve the garden in which all the fruits of life are cultivated. They would never have to go on the hunt for food when hunger called because the garden contained everything they could possibly need. They would also never have to labor for anything in order to take care of themselves.

While they were having fun, Theo was occupied with making sure Lilith would remember Adam for years to come. As time went on, Lilith developed a lust for her husband but was forbidden from wooing him. The reason for this is that Theo prohibited having sex on his sacred Elysian Plain. Theo's obedient Adam upheld the law and his divine commands, while Lilith put everything on the line to gain control. Theo gave her a vision of her future descendants while she sat beneath the fig tree by herself. She perceived herself as the mother of all the goddesses and gods in her vision. When she called Adam to ask for advice and an interpretation of her vision, he declined.

"Keep your thoughts to yourself because they contain the seeds of life. That is the result of your over-analyzing rather than a vision that Theo provided you." That were his reply to Lilith's plea, raising his bare body to face Lilith, and grasping the rod with his right hand. Then, as he turned to go, Lilith erupted from her spot on the cattle pelt, yelling, "I know that, but you can't draw the conclusion that they are my ideas! I need my feelings to be shared with you. I need your eyes to see what I see." She even went to her knees, putting her head on the man's leg and letting the tears fall so Adam would feel sorry for her. Gazing up into the sky, he thought that perhaps Theo might explain the vision he had given Lilith.

He exclaimed, "I see a strange cloud," as a peculiar cloud appeared. "Is that what you observed?" With his head still turned to look up at heaven, he questioned. She turned to face the sky in an attempt to see what her husband was showing her, but all she saw was a bright blue sky lit by the sun.

"All I see is the sun shining on a clear sky. The same event that occurred there also occurred here. Tell me what you observe." After responding, she got to her feet and moved to stand next to Adam, eager to hear about his vision. He observed the metropolis and a large number of kids playing on the cloud. "I see the families of Midgard, our descendant," was the reply given after that. "I apologize for being cruel to you by not offering to interpret your vision." He turned to face Lilith, who nodded in response. The discussion didn't seem to be getting any closer to being over.

Lilith frequently stated throughout their conversation beneath the fig tree that she wanted equal rights, autonomy, and control over her own life.

"Theo gave us the same vision for the future, so we have things that are comparable in shared ownership," Adam found her speech to be cryptic and needed further clarification on what she had said. He sensed from her discussion that she had a lot of requests, so he intended to ask her about them. "Why so many are clamoring for autonomy and freedom while you have free will to do as you please?" he questioned, holding her in his arms as they stood under the fig tree's shade on a sunny day. He also kissed her forehead. She examined him closely before responding, thinking that he would not be happy, but instead she saw a smile.

She then retorted, "This means that I have life, that I think, feel, speak, walk, dream, and most importantly, that I will be a mother to the descendants we shall bring." After uttering her statement, she went on, separating herself from Adam and leaving him holding hands. They were talking while they were both nude and they didn't feel embarrassed, like they were children. The man asked, "This sounds peculiar, tell me please what your request of me in seeing I am of the Lord as an advocate?" considering the remark the woman had made left him with a lot of questions. Lilith finally had the opportunity to express the feeling and vision she had been holding for a long time.

"Ask Theo to give us a romantic moment so we may show each other how we attach to one another and have concrete proof of our relationship. Let's see whether I'm unable to conceive our offspring." Her conversation with him demonstrated to him that although she had flirted with him, she was not allowed to have sex in any way in the hallowed Elysian Plain garden.

He answered, "I will talk to him for your love's sake," to console his wife. As if Theo, their creator, had heard that they were in need of him. With no more words spoken, Theo materialized in their midst, and they all dropped to their knees, and prostrated with their faces contacting the grass. Their kneeling was due to their belief that he was angry with them. Still, he was displeased by the identical gesture they made. Even their reverence for him demonstrated that they were unaware that he regarded them as more than just his creations—rather, they were his buddies and fellow gods.

"I had created you in my likeness and in my image. What manner of honor is this to your fellow friend?" he scolded them as they carried on paying homage to him. The woman found an opportunity to speak direct to Theo without any need for Adam to speak deliver her request. She smiled on her own while she was still prostrating with her face still on the ground and hands spread open.

"Pardon our iniquity my Lord, but your presence injects us with requests." she poured out her mind direct to Theo, her father who was stand on the cloud that stood before them with his dazzling appearance. The atmosphere became so gloomy as if it would rain storm.

Theo continued to speak with the bold voice as if it was the running waters, "what is your petition Lilith my daughter?" So kind was the tone of his strong voice as if he didn't know her request. The thundering and lightening followed. As asked, she had to respond even though she had fear.

"The ability to govern oneself." I therefore want to have the same authority as Adam; I want to be on par with him. You took us both from the dust of the earth and fashioned us into distinct individuals with unequal rights. It is a tough pill to swallow to live as a servant in my husband's shadow when one has power but no authority." As though voicing her wish would summon the hosts of Nirvana. Angels were now perched on the cloud pillar, covering the area where Theo had stood. Adam was aware of Lilith's violent nature and didn't want to become involved in any debates involving her. Theo answered her request, and he remained silent.

"He has power and dominion over Midgard as a whole, not just over you. I have given you the authority to assist him as my servant. Do you not feel content with being a woman?" After hearing his response, she boldly got up and turned to face him. Nevertheless, his dazzling appearance prevented her from seeing his face.

"I am happy but feel a bit small," she replied, still in a prostrate position. "Power will give me freedom and enable me to thrive inside the boundaries of Midgard, loving my children." Talking like a father and his daughter, Theo inquired, "Would you grant someone else the same desire as yours if you were in my shoes?"

"What a worthwhile inquiry?" Before she answered, she whispered within herself.

"Yes, I would, but under certain circumstances," she responded. Theo was charmed by his daughter's audacity and he laughed. The area where the gathering was taking place was now encircled by angels. Lilith, on the other hand, was directly facing Theo when he stated, "Tomorrow, if I give you independence, you'll ask me to add two more eyeballs to your back so you can see how your front and back look. You'll ask me to rearrange your bodily components and alter the way your skeleton is put together. You are not welcome here; I am the one who made you.

Adam was still savoring the moment of ease in his heart, but Lilith's attitude was clear—she was angry with Theo. The father and his daughter's argument has now escalated into an altercation. This is because Theo won't give Lilith what she really wants.

Then, yelling, "that means you created us for your own good not with purpose!" she blasphemed against him. "You claim that "we are your image and likeness," but you are self-centered and confine us. I'm sorry to tell it, but I am not going to stop until my wishes come true."

Theo lost his temper with Lilith, his daughter as well, and said, "Who are you without me? As a result of your arrogance, you believe that you are just like me, but in reality, you are nothing more than flesh made of earthly dust. Although I've granted you the freedom to be who you are, I won't bring back the hardships you have endured. I created you with the intention that you would give birth to human beings in the future, but now you disparage my creations while I'm still trying to accomplish my goals. You cause me to regret giving you these presents and turning my attention to you." Throughout her altercation with her father, the woman stuck to her word.

"Please excuse my selfishness, which turned into arrogance, but the feminist spirit had found its way inside me, " she answered. "It caused me to reflect on who I am, and I realized that I am an immortal goddess rather than merely a human." Through her statement, Theo now demonstrated his daughter's wisdom.

"Yes, I have overfed you with my glory alone, which is why pride has arisen within you and you exalt yourself above a male created in my image," the God, Theo remarked. Lilith asked, "Am I not created in your image too?" with her hands on her waste while she was still undressed, in reaction to Theo's statement.

Theo replied, "Nay, but you are created in my likeness as the only female in the universe that is what makes you demand independence. In all of my creation, you are engulfed in my glory and beauty. But you are just flesh forged out of the dust of the ground. That gives you no right to question me on any occasion."

Lilith appeal to Theo saying, "That makes me mortal, doesn't it? Supplement me with everlasting existence and I will submit to my husband." Theo's reasoning with Lilith made him feel as if the female would now take advantage of him. therefore, to threaten her was the only want to end her pride and silence her talk.

He replied, "Your existence is eternal but death lies by the door if you transgress my law and command. You shall be a vagabond wandering to and fro the realm of Midgard where your corpses will be wasted and I will strip you off my glory that ensconced you." The threats Theo made didn't move the female to be scared. This was proven by the broad smile on her face as she said, "I understand your reasoning, but I wish to exercise my primacy in my own realm." Seeing that Lilith was not threatened, he moved up while talking saying, "I have granted your heart desires ever since you were created." He then disappeared from the presence of his creation and the place where the talk was held was now sunny again as before.

Upon Theo's departure, Lilith rose to grapple with Adam. She insulted him for not backing her during her controversy with Theo saying, "But what kind of a male are you who doesn't back his female up. If you betrayed me to Theo for my demand for independence, you must be a traitor. You are an imbecile not a man of honor for me to submit to. I would rather wander Midgard alone than submit to you Adam. Surely you are on the side of Theo and pleased to see me grieve. Is it true that you seem to be among the quick and the dead? Did Theo prune you and forbid you from interfering in my skirmishes with him?" During her rebukes, Adam rose from the ground to face the shouting female. He had to defend himself from the altercation the woman had now just started with him.

He replied, "Nay, my wife; but Theo is constantly watching over us. How could I possibly betray you when I love you so much? You know you have free will to do as much as you need. Midgard is yours to possess but wait for Theo to establish you there first." Her facial expression proved her disapproving the statement Adam made. He ended up seeing that Lilith was taking advantage of him. Therefore, he sought to bring her on her knees. He talk with anger aiming at threatening the female saying, "without him we are vagabonds. You are puckish and your proud behavior makes me coy. Silence pleases my creator but your rebellion debilitates him from implementing his purpose concerning us. You are a disgrace before the angels of Nirvana!"

Lilith despised Adam, "your blasphemies won't change my plans and I know that Theo won't show me any benevolence to my sins. You are benighted and an object to my ridicule; I will defile your prowess." Lilith's threats provoked Adam and made him boil in anger against his wife. The first blow of the argument was aimed at slapping her with his left hand as he stood up from the ground where he knelt.

The wind of Theo evaded Lilith and drove her to the south side of Elysian Plain where she sat and mourned like a hermit and a banished feminist who lost caste with the Elysian Plain. She became invisible to Adam and all creation in Elysian Plain; only Theo and his archangel, Phosphorous could locate her because he was his right hand angel and the guardian of other angels.

2

The Banishment of rebellious Angels

Theo handed Adam dominion over the Elysian Plain as king, but as mankind began to grow envious of one another, the kingdom descended into chaos. The man became Lilith's prey, shattering the pact between the two, and the realm descended into chaos. Theo tried his hardest to win Lilith over to Adam and exercised his companionship to both of them with great fervor, but his efforts were unsuccessful.

This terrible disturbance occurred up until Nirvana's host found out, at which point the angels' level of unease increased.

Phosphorous, Theo's right hand, whose beauty was called the "morning star," found Lilith's boldness intriguing. Her call for independence served as the catalyst for the uprising that took place in Elysian Plain. He attempted to seize Theo's throne by studying her acting technique.

While Theo was focused on Adam and Lilith, he entrusted the angels and Nirvana in the hands of his guardian.

He led a large group of his angels eastward of Nirvana at dawn to see the sun rise, but he kept his purpose a secret from them. Gathered around Phosphorous, they sat in a circle as he explained to them Lilith's feminism and his plan to marry her.

"We were formed as only angels, with beauty and wisdom, but without the ability to build or destroy," he declared. Now look, the universe's only woman had rebelled against Theo and was left on her own. In return for her strength,

I would like to take her on as my wife and grant her wisdom."

The angels gave him a hearty round of applause and expressed their desire to see his proposal carried out—but only under Theo's direction.

"Isn't this self-exaltation which will make us your worshipers?" inquired one of the angels. "Before you rebel against our creator, Phosphorous, consider what you have to say. We will always be angels and never be Theo, even if we are envious of him."

With the words, "Your weakness should not interfere with our plot," Phosphorous declared his superiority. "I am the unfathomably wise guardian of yours. I am a god, not just an angel. Nirvana is under my total control, and her beauty reflects my own."

The plot that Phosphorous was developing angered several angels. They attempted to return to their dwellings because they were afraid of rebelling against Theo.

Phosphorous, however, apprehended, tormented, and killed them. Afterwards, they left Nirvana without Theo's consent, and Theo noticed. He summoned the second-in-command archangel Michael, and encased him in armor by putting his seal on the sword he wields in combat.

"Be careful not to form an alliance with Phosphorous because I have made up my mind to banish him from Nirvana," he remarked to him. "He exalts himself and forgets that he is only an angel with no authority like Adan or strength like Lilith because of his beauty, which is why I have discovered evil in him.

"Don't you think he will form an alliance with Lilith, who envied you, and work to afflict Adam if you banish him?" Michael responded back. "Since Adam is the only lamb you have, please consider him to be your shepherd."

Michael was appealed to by Theo, who said, "Let's get rid of the workers of iniquity. I hear your request and will consider him too." My kingdom is Nirvana, which is currently a center of disobedience."

So, with the army of angels behind him, Michael entered the battle. When Phosphorous saw him approaching, he called out to his group, "Your god is coming." I'll put him to death as well." Nevertheless, he saw uncertainty in his soldiers' eyes as they began to quake upon hearing him warn them of the impending clash. As Michael reached the battlefield, the combat formation was being readied. Every angel had a flaming sword in his hand and their bodies were covered in regal flaming garments. Although the numbers on both sides seemed equal, Michael had his father, Theo on his side. It was therefore conceivable for him to win. Michael informed Phosphorous about his fate later on during the combat formation.

He declared, "The Lord has taken into account your future and has created you a vagrant who will spend all of eternity roaming around the garden of Sorrow. You have lost who you are and elevated yourself. I would want to remind you that you are merely an angel possessing no strength or ability, but rather a wise man."

"Pardon me, my servant, but a woman with beauty like Nirvana has tempted me and I am tempted to establish a love affair and come back with her power," Phosphorous said in response, finding his comment amusing. "Don't you also want to be married to her?" He said that, and then he laughed.

"I am an angel, not a man, therefore I don't have feelings as men do," Michael remarked in response. "Do you feel anything for her?" The conversation that took place between the two opposing angels appeared to be about Lilith, the woman, and her boldness in demanding autonomy.

Then Phosphorous made fun of Michael by stating, "She will have dinner with me tonight in Theo's paradise." I'll arrange a marriage ceremony and bring your head to the table. "My alcohol to get intoxicated will be a cup full of your blood." Their father was watching while the two leaders traded threats. He intended to find out what his trusted son, Michael would do to his sibling, Phosphorous.

Michael answered, "I will catch you, fasten you, and put an iron yoke on you and your host so that the Lord may judge you." He will take you from his glory and banish you from his presence. Then you will be judged by your own beauty, which elevated you, and you will be a son of the night rather than the light. Your followers will be demons with faces resembling those of wild animals and dragons, and you yourself will be an evil monster and the son of the devil." His father Theo laughed at what he said. He went so far as to nod his head and tell himself, "This is my son, and I am proud of him." I count on him in any way."

But Phosphorous was inflamed, and they engaged in combat. Phosphorous attacked Michael at the start of the battle, not realizing that he was carrying his father's sword. It took a long time for Michael to overcome Phosphorous in the struggle. The fact that he was able to keep his word proved this. He led him before Theo so that Theo might judge him after tying him up with the shackles that caused him to lose his strength.

He curses Theo, stating, "I am of perfect beauty like the dawn and you are just a spirit," as he steps up before Theo's throne. "I sit on God's throne given that I am God. I am free to do anything I need to as much as I desire. I possess a higher level of intelligence than Lilith, your spouse, the feminist who advocates for autonomy. After she disgraced your omnipotence and made fun of your godliness, how are you feeling now? See if I can resist using her power to come mock you for all of eternity. I own all you have created because you are evil. I'll create a new Nirvana and invite you to stay with me." As he kneeled before his father's throne, he uttered these words. Behind him stood Michael, clutching the chains that bound Phosphorous at the wrist, foot, and neck.

Theo answered, "If you had enough strength you would not be bound and brought to me," as the angels peered at him to see what he would do with those who planned revolt." You have an evil heart, though, and I will never be able to restore you to your throne because of this. I have cast you off my throne today, and you will now roam aimlessly without any place to call home."

Phosphorous and his entourage of disobedient angels were judged by Theo. He drove them out of Nirvana, leaving his seat unoccupied to his right. They heard a tremendous weeping during their time in banishment. A few angels grew wary of following Phosphorous. They sobbed, pleading for pardon. Together, we said, "We have been duped by our leader." We are not able to live like the wanderer he has become. Give us one last chance, under the guidance of your reliable leader, to demonstrate who we are." The entrance to Nirvana was wide open for the disobedient angel to leave, so Theo covered his face in response to their cries so that Michael would show them no mercy. When Theo shot the doors of nirvana against them, they had no idea what would happen to them. But Theo forced Phosphorous out of Nirvana with a powerful cloud that was mixed with thunder and lightning. Phosphorous was unable to stop Theo's force from ejecting him from Nirvana in all of his tries. He became aware of how dark the area outside Nirvana's doors was. He was aware that rebelling against his father was a mistake. Before Theo's energy propelled him out of Nirvana, he let out one more cry.

"What kind of a father are you that you do not have any mercy for your beloved sons?" he said. "Why don't you banish me on my own and let your angels join you?" Since he was now hidden from Phosphorous, Theo responded to his comment through the cloud, saying, "They will be your guest at your wedding with Lilith."

"However, I'm an angel. How do I marry a woman?" He spoke as if he was suddenly regretting his words. He said this while he hesitated to exit Nirvana's door. Theo didn't reply to it, though. Michael considered responding to him, though, by stating, "As you have stated, you will host your marriage in Theo's paradise." Thus, invite your team of revolt as guests and host it in the void." Michael ended his dialogue with Phosphorous, and the cloud transported Phosphorous and his group out of Nirvana. Theo then closed the doors behind them, preventing them from pleading with him to see him again. Michael went back to Theo, but Phosphorous was welcomed as his son by the dark void. After he ascended to his kingdom, a lavish party was held to mark Michael's triumph over the rebels. Angels sung while dancers performed to the tune of trumpets and other humorous noises.

While joy was being experienced in Nirvana, sorrow was being felt in the void where Phosphorous and his rebels had submerged. It appeared as though they were lamenting the loss of their ability to reach Nirvana. Nonetheless, their beauty caused them to shine in the gloomy space. So they continued looking for Lilith, until eventually they discovered her in her grief by alone in the southern part of the Elysian Plain garden, where night and day are usually found. The realm, known as Midgard, is inhabited by godlike humans who possess the same creation and destruction powers like Theo.

3

Lilith Abandons Elysian Plain

The Angels became fearful after Phosphorous was banished from Nirvana, and Theo appointed Michael, the Archangel to keep an eye on heaven as a whole. His actions were perfect, and the status quo was reinstated. This brought Phosphorous to ruin, and he wandered around with a host of angels. He was full of plans to take revenge on Theo, and his rage was escalating. One of his angels reminded him of Lilith during his time spent roaming across the void, and together they looked for her until they discovered her by herself beneath a fig tree south of the Elysian Plain. Lilith felt his presence close to her, and she was instantly terrified. "I stand in the name of Theo, my father," she shouted as she got up to further insult the void. "I give you the order to reveal yourself as a coward hidden in the shadows." Indeed, Phosphorus appeared before her as though he were descending like Theo did to see Lilith and Adam in a cloud. Lilith believed that Theo had dispatched angels to come get her. She was relieved when Phosphorous said, "Let a god restore it, as the soul of a stone sinks in a deep lake." "You had been fearful due to Theo's threats."

As a result, your property may become barren of greenery and the cattle may starve as the rain stops, and the greenery will wither." You take a gulp of your well's harsh waters." Phosphorous stood before Lilith with his angels encircling him, and his words were so lovely that even Lilith's concerns were allayed. Lilith continued nodding her head as if she agreed with every word that came out of the phosphorous's mouth. Lilith answered, "Speak on, angel, I am listening and hoping you have not come to bring me back to my dumb husband, Adam," in response to his speech. Phosphorous smiled as a result of her words, and he stepped toward her. However, she retreated, seemingly fearful of him, but he still knelt in front of her and said, "How long will you grieve without someone to comfort you? How much longer can you bear the suffering caused by Theo's yoke? Do we not have a common blood? Before we are dumped into a hole filled with the blood of dead soldiers to maintain grief on the face of our seed, let us celebrate for a little while, the fruits of our own labors." Lilith continued to stare down at him while he faced her and spoke in a way akin to a guy proposing to his spouse.

Then he got up and covered Lilith with the royal robe that was on him. The woman remarked, "I am grateful for this," observing the fallen angel's concern. "Tell me, please, who you are." Phosphorous gave a nod of his head before getting down on his knees like previously. "I am the Guardian of the angels of Theo and I have come so that even your oppressor can be your friend," he said, deceiving her despite distorting the facts.

Fearing for her life, Lilith questioned Phosphorous, "What's your heritage barbarian that made you come over to my realm?"

"I am the Guardian of the angels of Theo in Nirvana," Phosphorous assured her, denying the reality. I come to join you in bringing about peace. Here I am, Lilith, the fine linen, the freedom's reflection in a tranquil region under seraphim watch. Your attire is one of honor and strength, enabling your generation to speak wisely and with pure hearts when their time finally arrives." The two seemed to understand each other as they exchanged the enigmatic remarks. Lilith responded to his speech by saying, "My soul is grieving as a result of my envy and desire for independence." I feel that my favor with Theo has been taken away now.

Are you attempting to make things better between us?" The fallen angel revealed his true identity in response to her inquiries. In response, he said, "I feel dissatisfied by whatever he tastes, and he expelled me from Nirvana. His severe laws are founded on absolute authority. I now want my uncertain circumstances to be restructured, together with a pristine land and the virginity of my destiny. My intention is to venture into the world of evil and craft as many schemes as possible to attack both Nirvana and Elysian Plain. I shall apply my wisdom to uphold the concepts of Theo's creation's oneness and freedom." As he spoke on, his angels fell silent and began to sing.

"I create a strategy based on the knowledge I obtained as an ordained powerful guardian to put men in my hands to serve me," he said.

"I wonder how would that be accomplished, seeing as Theo is monitoring every move his children make?" Lilith questioned about his plans for completing the task. "Then he would craft my boards from fir trees and my masks from their oaks in the magnificent Elysian Plain," he continued.

"After the war, they will construct my oars with their blood. Their exquisite linen laced with lace broided will envelop me.

Disperse it around Theo's inn and upper realms to build my honor in Midgard. They will be my pilots and mariners, and together they will restock the lands' splendor with the sale of private boats and warships. I shall ride up to my celestial throne and insult and dishonor Theo as a result of their planes. I will shake the thrones of Nirvana to perpetual restlessness with iniquity, regardless of their piety. Given that the gods are more powerful than I am, my army will be constructed with all of their might. They will hang their shields and lay their spears over my head for an everlasting alteration to their life in disguise after every fight, whether they win or lose.

So I'll use their composure to justify my jealousy. They will present me as a powerful protector, using their powers to drive out all evil.

I shall start fierce fights in order to seize their riches as trophies. I'll turn their businesses into my merchants and force them to transact with all of Nirvana's wealth.

I shall sow jealousy among the people of all colors, allowing the powerful to engage in trade with the weak in order to create division, as my gadget cannot be finished without power." Lilith was so taken aback by Phosphorous's declaration. She realized he was talking about the offspring she would raise. "Are you now talking about my offspring I would bare to Adam?" she inquired. He is no longer my spouse because Theo broke us up."

"I see them trading at my fair with modern horses and riding on horseback amidst eternal wars, with the perception of peace existing only in their imagination and absent from the market," he said, answering her inquiry. They will trade wheat, honey, oil, and all the other unspecified food items in my fair and sell them in my market of grief. As a sacrifice, they will give me their blood in exchange for all the resources they have been fed. They will dress my victory in priceless clothing.

Lilith said, "You are talking mystery, what do you mean?" after realizing the cryptic talk of Phosphorous. he then realized at this point that he had gained the woman's heart. He got up from the spot he was kneeling on and walked around the female, talking. "Nay, but I shall force Adam to violate Theo's divine instruction which would allow me to access the riches of Elysian Plain," he said as he went on. The woman thought his strategy looked risk-free but good. "Don't you fear that a new king shall be discovered and declare war against you?" she questioned as a result.

"Nay, but I'll get Adam to break Theo's rules so I can get his wealth," he retorted. "Look at the gold-filled rivers that flow through the Elysian Plain. Saying, "We are sinking like stones in a lake, but my seed refuses to accept it," Lilith began to join the angel in declaring and cursing Theo. "I was filled with fear and terror as a result of vast troops that caused a lush region to become dry. Because the rain will no longer fall on my farm, my animals may get hungry and the grass may not flourish."

I don't want to drink the waters from her wells because the plants and fruit trees have dried up from their roots and are so bitter. How long will I grieve in silence and without support? How much longer will I put up with my yoke of living in the spotlight of men? Tell me, Phosphorous, are our bloods not the same?"

Phosphorous retorted as he kept circling the female, "Yes, we are one blood of one creator who is now celebrating because we have been slain and spiritual death has befallen us," . Let's work together to find a new territory so that we may claim it as our own." The female was unaware that the angel need her power in order to complete his goal. Now, her thoughts were no longer on Adam and Theo. She began to make plans to accompany Phosphorous on his wandering. So she just listened to what he had to say.

"I announce that in order to exact revenge on our father and instill peace inside us, I will join forces with you and combine my knowledge with your strength. Well, here I am, Lilith! Let us be like the beautiful linen in a tranquil area that is watched over by Theo, the holy one." "Strength and honor you dress so your generation may rejoice at the appearance of their time and speak wisdom with a clean tongue in the law of kindness," he said, starting to bless and adore her. Whoa! Isn't Lilith the serenity of spirit that maintains a man on his feet? Oh, you're doing great! Lilith, so that the offspring of Adam may honor you, and women may accept feminism and be granted happiness as spouses.

They are going to bless you with gifts. Both within and outside of your inn, blessings await you." That's when she learned that even the fallen angel respected her might. Theo watched out while they conversed. He would even share the correspondence from Michael laughter. This is because he was aware of his scheme to imprison Phosphorous in the domain of hell and return Lilith to Adam, her spouse, in Elysian Plain.

"Your generation shall use words as a two-edged sword against the trespassing tongues that impose unjust laws to keep the just in captivity," Phosphorous said in a speech Theo heard. "But once more, I declare, "I am the oppressor's god."

With his depraved treatment of the slaves, he worships me, and his jealous heart flaunts my cunning. He licks my face's perspiration and slumbers at my feet. It is inevitable that I will become enlightened with a feminine force beyond Nirvana and ascend to a throne beyond Theo."

Following Lilith's consent to be questioned by Phosphorous in front of the angels, the league was formed. She went with Phosphorous and their angels, leaving Elysian Plain behind and traveling back and forth through Midgard.

She was no longer bound by the confines of Elysian Plain, and life seemed more comfortable. Contrary to other angels, she was without wings. couldn't fly like Phosphorous and angels as a result, but instead, she would visualize the location she wanted to travel, then show up there and accomplish her goals.

Because she was a goddess rather than an angel, the angels revered her and feared her greatly. In Elysian Plain, she and Adam live in a world where they can have anything they desire without having to work hard, travel far, or take public transportation.

They would just image their destination and materialize there without having to travel, or they would think what they desired and appear to it and perform what they wanted.

4

The man mourns for his wife

When his wife disappears and is never again his, a guy truly understands how deeply he loves her. The man was quite anxious till he arrived on the mountain, reminiscing Lilith and dreaming of their future together as the first humans. He decided to relax on a golden rock in the midday heat on the tall hill of the Elysian Plain as there was nothing else around. Like a furnace, this is scorching.

"I feel an absolute agony at the loss of my wife," he said, reflecting on his future without a spouse. Where did she ultimately end up? What direction should one go—north, south, east, or west? How should I go about finding her?

Lilith, who was made with me from the ground's dust and given life, is someone I never imagined would be snatched from me. Who can lessen my regrets, since my soul is vanishing? I am a hermit today, but I was a husband yesterday.

Seeing my future unfold before my eyes is the most unsettling thing for me. A dream concerning the Midgardians.

Is it my fault that she left? I never intended to be the reason behind her leaving the Elysian Plain and me. Each of us was given responsibility over Theo's domain in Elysian Plain.

I can't stand this scenario, but will Theo be able to track her down for me so that we can make amends and begin over in harmony and peace?

My capacity to grant her the independence she demands while I carry out my manly duties is infused with love and compassion. She is the embodiment of my conception of beauty.

Is it because she expected my support during her altercation with Theo, and I relished the stillness that moment? However, she was a little disrespectful and vindictive against him. Moreover, she was mistrustful of me, and I took no action—neither sensible nor stupid—to stop her plan.

No life, no women for me. I have no one to entertain me like she used to. Nobody to cheer me up and declare that I am worthy of her praise.

I am buried beneath ground zero, despite having been branded a hero. Is it my fault or Theo's that I'm in this situation? Please excuse me, but I am grieving for Lilith, and Theo has a purpose.

I would have someone to love, someone to energize me, and someone to talk to if she were here. I cherish her affection the most because it was meaningful.

She has since vanished. I used to find solace in her gentleness when I was grieving. I have no one to comfort me while I grieve right now. I wonder what fate has in store for her. What worries me is that she will become the mother of mankind."

Theo was watching over Adam from above from his vantage point in Nirvana during his entire period of grieving. He promised to establish his presence in him if Lilith failed him entirely, and as a result of Lilith's failure, he sent three angels to console him. He was confronted by them, and the first angel, Sepoy, materialized atop a shadowy cloud that obscured the sun that Adam was basking in. "The Lord is with you, mighty man of valor," he said as he appeared to the man. "Let go of your tears, for the Lord has heard your lamentations and will fulfill your request. Please let us know so we can get back to him."

In shock, Adam mistakenly believed Sepoy to be Theo. This is due to the fact that he had a dazzling appearance similar to Theo's angels. He remained reclined on the ground, nevertheless, and did not get up. Even though Adam's memories of the light were obscured by the cloud that Sepoy stood atop. "Please locate me, Lilith," he murmured. "I want her returned to me when you have searched the depths of Midgard. Declare that I will fulfill all of her wishes.

Reacting to Adam."

Then Sepoy stated that "As per your word, we will look for her, but let us first consult Theo. The riot that happened in Elysian Plain also happened in Nirvana." Suddenly, Nirvana has become a chaotic battleground, but Theo remains holy. Behold, oh Adam, the lamb of Theo.

Nirvana experienced the same uprising that had occurred on the Elysian Plain. The battle had been won by the sons of Theo, and numbers of angels had been driven out. I'll tell you the truth: enjoy being alone since it will give Theo ample opportunity to get to know you, become friends, and establish you as a fellow god of Elysian Plain."

"Peace be unto you," Sepoy soothed him further. "If Lilith says no, she's not coming back to you; the wife of your type will be on her way to meet you. Theo goes through the same pains as you do.

Recently, there was a riot when Theo's heir apparent, the protector of the angels, rebelled against him. He protected his host and served as his right hand. Although what happened was unintentional, we can choose to go on with our lives and carry out our future plans, or we can remain in grief indefinitely."

Adam then realized it was Theo's scheme to produce another woman for him. "I believe Theo ought to create another female to ease my sorrow, determine my fate, and even accomplish Theo's dream," he remarked.

"If by tomorrow we don't bring Lilith to you, know that Theo is working on bringing to you a female who is obedient and will submit to you and follow your command," Sepoy stated, clearly sensing that Adam was having a heated discussion.

They made plans for how they were going to go throughout Midgard. Saying, "We intend to confer with the Lord over your desire to bring Lilith back to Elysian Plain, what should we say to him in response? Describe your heart's condition for us. Are you as sober as the Elysian Plain's well-water, or are you in high spirits?

"I'm not in a healthy state since it's difficult for me to tell whether I'm okay or not," Adam said as he stood up from the ground. "I will grieve for what I had lost all over again if I stay by myself during this period and the years that follow. But I shall be sober and I will praise the Lord if my wish comes true and Lilith comes back to me. I am somewhere between day and night, I tell you now."

Sepoy realized that this was not the response he would give his father in Nirvana. Even though Adam was benighted and just needed his wife to return, Sepoy was aware that Theo was listening in on their conversation at this moment. "We cannot bring that response to the Lord," he replied, adding, "but we will inform him only of your desire to search and return Lilith to Elysian Plain."

Thus, we won't come back until we locate her or until Theo personally spends time with you so that you can feel better if we were unable to console you.

"Go back to him so he can give you permission to enter Midgard and look for my wife," Adam retorted. "Here's what you should do when you meet Lilith. If you can, bow down or prostrate yourself before her. Your admiration will make her laugh, and she'll believe that Theo has come to give her the power she wants.

Should she inquire, "What kind of respect do you exhibit?"

Inform her that you have been dispatched by me, Adam, to return her to Elysian Plain. She is now in a position of authority and is ranked above me because of this. Say to her, "I am ready and willing to greet her and make her feel comfortable as she leads with joy and fear."

"We will ask Theo if this is in line with his plan for you," Sepoy responded, shaking his head. "The symbol of worship that you want us to bring in is forbidden by the Lord." So that we can find out where and when to look for Lilith, let's go back to the Lord. Adam was reassured that the angels had left him when he witnessed Theo step in.

As angels began to ascend to Nirvana, he was left sitting on the gold stone he had been lying on and staring up at the sky.

5

The formation of a new spouse

When Theo's angels who had been sent to comfort Adam returned, he inquired them about their well-being as though he hadn't been watching their argument with Adam, and they brought up Adam's request.

"Your son mourns for his wife who vanished from Elysian Plain," said Sepoy as he spoke. "He wants us to take her back to the Elysian Plain and guarantee that she will have everything she wants when she gets there."

"Her birthright has been darkened and the light in Elysian Plain has been covered by the shadows of the northern hills," Theo retorted. "She wants to hurt my kid, Adam and myself due to her evil is so great. I would have to return Phosphorous' right hand if I were to bring her back to the Elysian Plain.

But I am not able to, thus Lilith cannot remain attached to Adam.

But in order to assist him, I shall use his body to construct a new wife. So that she may tell him all she wants, she would carry me inside her body. Undoubtedly, it is improper for a guy to be left alone; I will make arrangements for him to meet someone.

Her humility will force her to yield to him, and I'll arrange for them to support one another."

As Theo replied, Sepoy, still kneeling before his throne, questioned, "You mean we shouldn't search for Lilith just to find out about her dwelling places and her welfare?"

In response, Theo said, "She's in the east of Midgard." They intend to attack Elysian Plain and take away my son's glory, as I can see. "Tell Adam that I am following you immediately when you return. I am going to present him with a woman made of his own bones and flesh."

She is going to be a woman whose heart will be toward him. Regarding Lilith, I will deliver her from Phosphorous's deceit, split them apart, and incite hostility between them. He will become a devil, and I will later restore Lilith to her mother's womb. She will resurrect, and I will establish her in the human race."

The angels left Theo's presence in Nirvana and materialized in front of Adam in the Elysian Plain. He was sitting where he had been positioned. He got up and began to fidget around the angel as soon as he noticed them next to him.

Sepoy said, "We have good news for you, Adam," but Adam was expecting to see the angels he had sent to bring Lilith back so he was able to feel at home with his wife. He was taken aback to see them by themselves without his wife.

"I hope you're not kidding right?" he inquired. You did say you wouldn't come back if you couldn't locate Lilith, didn't you? Theo has decided to send you; he used to come down to visit me for fellowship. Why? Does this mean that my creator and buddy have sent you? As for Lilith, where is she that I asked you to get for me?"

"Theo knew that you and him would not get along since your heart is still broken. But his eyes are still on you, not the woman. The spirit of the Lord will come and encircle you as soon as we leave you, so that you will believe that we are the messengers of the Lord.

"After that, you'll slip into a deep sleep, and when you awaken, someone new of your sort will be brought to you. As for Lilith, don't weep any longer; she has gone away and made a covenant with the enemies of the Lord." In response to Adam's query, Sepoy stated.

Adam then inquired, "Who are the adversaries of the Lord?"

Sepoy answered, "The right hand of Theo rebelled against the Lord, just as Lilith did. Phosphorous is the angel's guardian. Then there was a serious conflict in Nirvana, which led to the Lord's judgment and Phosphorous's exile.

He roamed around Midgard until your ex-wife, Lilith, allied herself with him.

As I speak, she is with him, and the plan to invade the Elysian Plain and make you emaciated is being fashioned. Because wickedness has been discovered in Lilith, the Lord will not approve your request to have her returned to Elysian Plain. Look up to Theo, I tell you, and he will mend the scars in your heart." When the angel finished speaking, the man was ecstatic.

Adam complimented Theo, "You speak like Theo, you have instructed me to embrace my humility and I am now strengthened from my weaknesses," Your words have reinforced my wobbly knees and lifted my sinking soul. Lilith had sown evil and plowed iniquity; what would she now have to harvest?

At Elysian Plain and in Adam, let Theo's will be done.

I'm his, and I'll do everything he wants, so he may do whatever he wants with me. Whether my future will ever be restored or my destiny determined is a very tough decision to make."

Sepoy then stated, "You will undoubtedly be the father of all humanity. The woman who will become your wife will bear sons and daughters, and your offspring will replenish Midgard. For the sake of Theo, we shall defend this territory."

After the messengers left Adam, the Lord's spirit enveloped him, comforting him. Adam then slipped into a deep sleep and Theo made the decision to construct a woman.

In order to create a female being that is Adam's kind, he removed two ribs from Adam's body. Following that, he enclosed him and created the woman. Afterwards, he awoke from a profound slumber with a surreal feeling. Theo then presented Adam with the female.

And when he looked up, he saw that his own flesh and bone were in front of him.

With his hands lifted in a blessing, Adam knelt down and said, "You empower me when I'm weak and trembling, and you strengthen me when I'm shifted from my position."

"It is you who will change people. Meliorism is what I believe. Beyond only being a man I can trust, you are also honest and trustworthy.

You have given me faith, and I will dedicate a chapter and verse to the lady you made me for the sake of future generations. I will call the woman you gave me Eva since she will be my offspring's mother.

As a result, please accept my sincere gratitude and I entrust you with Lilith's situation so that you can keep a watch on her. Eva, however, has inherited my affection for her, and I plan to continue this tradition with my next generation. My father, you have my blessing and my gratitude for watching over me. I am afraid of your affection, but I am committed to your trust."

Adam got to his feet from where he was kneeling.

He gave his freshly created wife a blessing, gave her hugs, and they grinned at each other while he held Eva. They were completely obscured from view by a storm cloud and lightning, leaving them only able to see each other.

As Theo began to love the woman he made for his son, his voice emerged from the ominous cloud and the rainbow's colors began to flash.

Theo spoke lovingly to the newly formed female, saying, "I have granted the woman I have called to help you the oddment of Nirvana."

"She is obligated to follow your lead by me, but it does not give you authority to use her. Your romantic connection will be ruined by it. She will obey your orders and take your call if you respect her status. She is going to feel important and cherished, and her day and night will be predicted.

But now that she is a new creation, her lack of knowledge has left her benighted. Admire her attractiveness since that's what she finds most appealing.

Adam said as he followed the instructions, "I love her and promise to do so as you have instructed me." I've given my soul license to do whatever makes her happy. This is definitive proof that I shall keep an eye on her water intake and outflow in the garden of her soul.

Since she was made of my own flesh and bone, I will undoubtedly greet daybreak with a grin as a sign of gratitude for the day." The newly created female thought this was her chance to say something as well. In response, she said, "My dearest man in need of your comfort, I salute you with my gracious attitude, with pains and grief of the past buried deep inside." If you accept my wishes, I will genuinely transform your palace into my own and, as your queen, I will improve its adornment and décor for the king.

Inform the queen of your plans for the day. Since you are graduating with that degree and I am your angel for the day, let me declare your well-being." Now, the father and his children were happily conversing with each other. Theo's admiration for the female and his advice to Adam on how to keep her happy made this evident. He stated in his speech saying, "Her desire for you shall be all women's desires for their love ones in your generation." Protection, please grant this to her in the future. Since you are her haven, she will need to be shielded and cuddled up in your arms every night. I am a spirit that comes to see you, but I cannot give her the physical comfort you should.

She surrenders to you, your majesty, for you are her shepherd. I am your fellow countryman, and you are her bodyguard and entourage.

Someone is not there to provide her with security outside of your warmth, protective wing. For all of eternity, she needs you by her side. She doesn't feel comfortable without you at her side all the time, thus she needs your protection. She needs time to really appreciate and love you.

Given how much you already have in common, money will be all you need to finance your property and get ready for future expectations. She requires shelter. Because Elysian Plain is small enough for you to take advantage of each other, it is a place of delight for the time being rather than a place to multiply."

Adam stated in answer to Theo's admonition to his son, "I want to prove my loyalty to her in exchange for her faith." I'll give her prophecies about her accomplishments throughout the day, telling her how amazing she is and how the world is reflected in her.

When I bring up marriage, our father will have to step in. I suppose it's not your turn just now; all I want is Eva and myself. I am aware that you and I both long for childrearing as well as enjoying sex, don't we?"

Theo retorted, "That's what you have in common."

Adam prayed saying, "Lead us, Lord, to your paradise so that we may eat in your host's presence." In our connection, our goal is to make each other happy. Alongside me, I want her to be content. I want you to know that my love for her is unconditional, unending, and real.

With reference to his spouse Eva, he remarked, "Come get my support, you need it when you are hindered. When you are stuck, I am your support."

Theo stated, "I made her to help you in your hour of need,"

Turning to face the newly made female Eva, Adam said, "Come and get it now, my love."

Surprised and beaming, Eva sent Theo off with a heart full of love for humanity. When they smiled and made a slow dance gesture toward one another, a darkness yet hung over them both.

"I will cover your publicly exposed dirty linen with my glory if you can fully comply with the list of things I requested above. Since heat is in my nature, I shall make your winter transform into summer. Your insecurities will be concealed by my bright attire, and you will find comfort in my bosom whenever you grieve." Said she.

6

Trapped in hell

Lilith and Phosphorous, the fallen angel, were searching Midgard for a suitable place to settle. Eva was formally welcomed into the world of the Elysian Plain at this point by Theo and Adam. Lilith lacked wings and was unable to fly because she is a human, even though other angels were soaring beside their protector, Phosphorous.

Still, she would picture their location every day, and she would show up there before angels even showed up. She therefore didn't try to go anywhere or do anything. Rather, she would perceive it or manifest in it and act in her own will. That was the spirit she shared with Adam on the Plain of Elysium, the Elysian Plain.

The angels should have worshipped her because she was not just any average wanderer but a goddess, the strongest person alive.

When she finally located her home, she saw herself in an underworld region under Midgard. In a fraction of a second, she was standing before this realm, yet she could not pass through.

The domain she called Hell, where the vagrants reside and where damnation and agony are experienced, was expected to have a wicked vibe.

"This place of business is a trap that Theo set. Until Phosphorous proves me correct or incorrect, I cannot pass." As she kept watching the establishment, "take on a ball-like form in a circle," she whispered to herself. Inside, the din was created by the myriad of singing birds.

It appears that the texts surrounding it described how fire and darkness turned everything good into evil and barred her from entry. When Phosphorous and his angels first came, they were fascinated with the realm and immediately desired to take possession of it.

The plan was for Phosphorous and his angels to be tormented and transformed into demons in order to take away their rights and beauty. They were to suffer from constant captivity and torture.

He inquired, approaching Lilith and standing by her side, "What do you think of this new Elysian Plain?" Since we are nomads, should we establish this as our new home?"

"I'm not allowed to enter this priceless land of perpetual fire fame," Lilith declared, knowing full well that it was a trap designed to torture the fallen angels. She added in her talk saying, "this world is designed for fallen angels with a lot of menace and disobedience, like you. The intention is to rid them of their resentment and malice."

The wise angel was overcome by foolishness and was forced to test the depths of hell.

"Let us prove your doubt," he said. "There are numerous boundaries surrounding the person you were created to be. We are going to treat this world as the home of the dead, and we are going to worshiped by the descendants of Adam. We are going to give them a fresh heart as a punishment, so they will continue to rebel against Theo day and night until he stops believing in him. We will adjudicate Adam's life and sentence him to an infernally hot furnace.

Theo's heart will be broken by this, and we will be referred to as the avengers taking revenge on our creator for leaving us. I'll make fun of him every day and make sure he never gets any rest at all.

Lilith saw then that the angel no longer liked her. She said in response, "You want to learn more about Hell? Please let me know if you think it's as fascinating as it appears."

Phosphorous summoned his army, and they marched across Hell without fear of the evil that was awaiting them. Similar to military personnel wearing royal robes as they matched in the direction of the thrones that were in front of them. Then, Phosphorous began to appreciate the establishment's beauty, which was greater on the inside than the outside. He even told his fellow angel that, "Lilith is not the supreme being she had believed her to be, but rather as weak as a woman. A fear of going inside such an establishment. We now question whether she would ever want to be our friend." Then he laughed, and Lilith heard him, though she stayed outside to wait. She believed that they were having fun indoors. But because she was so delighted she considered breaking her vow to Phosphorous.

one of the angels then inquired, "Can we tell her about the magnificence of this establishment? She had asked us to return the word to her." Phosphorous bowed his head, intending to send Lilith inside with one of his angels. Then he said, "yell for her to enter." Yes, the angel cried out, and the entire realm seemed to echo him. They believed that they were hearing a response in his exact words. The environment still echoed with their constant laughter. Lilith believed they had all been driven insane. The way they laughed is the reason for this. she yelled at them, "Are you guys okay?" She was shouting outside the establishment, but they were unable to hear her.

She believed that since she was a goddess and a woman rather than a man like the other members of her team, she had been left outdoors alone. She made the decision to violate her commitment to the deal and her covenant with Phosphorous after the angels failed to appear.

"I am breaking the covenant that I made with the angels," she declared in her statement. I am not an angel; I am a goddess and a woman. The Elysian plain is left to a divinity like me. How is my husband doing, I wonder? I miss him terribly, but we aren't together anymore. I wonder if Theo didn't find a woman that is similar to me to take my place." After that, she waited till she felt embarrassed of herself.

She traveled east of Midgard to spend time in a Shinar cave. She turned it into her own self-made haven. This is due to the fact that she was the only woman ever made on Earth before Theo introduced Eva to Adam as his future spouse. She appeared in an imagined cave after fleeing hell and remained there.

Following Lilith's departure, Phosphorous parted the flame of fire perched above the golden throne.

The demon emerged, bringing with it the stench of rotting corpses and heat that enveloped the entire realm. Their bodies were in excruciating pain, and the entire realm's atmosphere turned malevolent.

Phosphorous was transformed into the devil, a personification of evil and the enemy of all good people, with hooves and horns among his many physical attributes. As the antithesis of everything right, this evil entity and his army of demons were going to continue to instill fear in individuals from all walks of life.

He evolved into an evil entity that now prowls the planet, creating havoc and engaging in combat with the forces of good. The Devil, a hideous winged being with three faces, was seen devouring a cunning sinner whose wings sent icy winds across Hell's territory.

He had assumed the appearance of the horned, tail-wielding, trident-wielding figure that has persisted into the current era.

He is largely to blame for the instability and corruption that currently plague the globe, having physically changed it. Some angels, on the other hand, were transformed into Phosphorous' children and were portrayed as evil spirits with gloomy faces.

And they endured such abhorrent treatment while imprisoned there that regret overwhelmed their hearts.

7

The Return of Lilith

Lilith could not have picked a more ideal setting for her stay in Midgard—especially in a lonely cave with no one to talk to. She and Adam are no longer together. Because of the broken pact, Phosphorous is now stuck in Hell and cannot be her fellow vagabond. This indicates that Phosphorous is now an evil spirit rather than an angel or her lover.

She finds that Midgard's environment is ever-changing, with seasonal weather forcing her to modify her way of life, which is one of the less enjoyable elements of her visit. She was alone herself and could only sing melodies in the morning along with the birds.

She chose to go back to her husband, submit to him, and follow his lead from the start. Begin a fresh life with Adam with the goal of ensuring Midgard's posterity. Eva was the last person she expected to stand in her way.

Theo was hiding her from Lilith, so she wasn't aware of her.

She just visualized Adam and materialized directly behind him, cradling Eva in his arms, since her mode of transportation cost her nothing.

They were left holding hands and closing their eyes as the black cloud that had enveloped them rose upward. Theo had closed Adam's discerning intellect and left him acting like a normal guy, so they were unaware that Lilith was behind them.

With a pure heart, Lilith observed them, determined not to be jealous of Adam and his ill-fated wife, Eva.

With a small smile, she swiftly came to terms with the fact that there was no other way to go back in time. She was no longer the lone woman in the universe, which was the reason for this.

Lilith said to Adam, "Congratulations, my husband Adam. It's amazing how quickly you've moved on with your life." Theo have sent a new wife to meet you, which you have found on my own behalf. I simply left my father because I was angry and I couldn't find what I needed from him. Who claimed I was unable to return?How could he not even think to ask me before finding you a new wife? He is so unreliable."

Adam eased out of Eva's arms and turned slowly to face Lilith. Her return knotted his nerves.

The man stated in response to her speech, "Because you chose to be a vagabond and wander to and fro all realms in the universe and abandoned your mandate." You decided to cruise with Theo's enemy, Phosphorous, who had rebelled against Theo in Nirvana, same as you had rebelled against Theo and me here on Elysian Plain. As disobedient kids, you both want to demolish Theo's domain and distract him from his task.

How could Theo consult with such a petty wanderer who is impolite and self-centered in every manner? I was crying at your absence, so he brought me this sweet woman to console me.

The Lord, along with the host of his Angels in Nirvana above, is my witness that I missed you terribly, Lilith. Not even a small bird to tell me about you could be found in my search for you. Lilith, where have you been and why have you returned?"

As tears streamed down her face, Lilith said, "I was traveling on a trip exploring the realm of Midgard hoping to have my desires of independence granted." I was wrong, and I now regret what I did. Phosphorous is a devil who is imprisoned in hell. He and I had a covenant, but it has since been broken and our relationship is no longer valid.

Since he is an angel and I am a human, our relationship could never work. I've come to make amends with you now." Though it appeared that it was too late for them to get back together, the man saw regret in his ex-wife. He reacted in response to her speech, "It is too late, Lilith. You see this innocent humankind over here? She is my wife." Eva smiled and waved her hand at Lilith since she observed their discussion without interfering. Adam continued after that in his talk saying, "she is here to take your place, accomplish Midgard's dream, and raise the next generation. I no longer feel the same way about you because my love has been given to her. She is made of my bone and flesh. She is therefore the bone of my bone and the flesh of my flesh. We live for each other because we have similar interests." Lilith came up with a scheme to divert Adam's attention.

"Unfortunately, I am neither flesh nor bone of yours, but I still love you," she said, expressing her affection for him. "If you put this woman first, I will stop at nothing to mend our differences as your first or second wives. Adam, since you and I were both formed from the dust of the earth, I submit to you as my leader and spouse. I want to spend time with you both here in Elysian Plain and I need a second chance.

I shall be a goddess hovering over you and your wife. We'll play together, talk, and discuss our dreams for the future. I have no issues at all with this stunning woman who is benighted. She is my identical replica in terms of beauty and heart.

I plead for another chance to thrive on the Elysian Plain because, Adam, for I love your wife, Eva too and I will never hurt her. I don't have a place to call home, and not all of my wants are met." The woman seemed remorseful and in need of another chance to show her ex-husband how much she loved him, and the man sympathized with her. Even when there's a newly made female to take her place. Adam retorted, "Only Theo can decide about your fate, but as for me, since you promise to never do any harm to Eva, my wife, then that settles it." I give you permission to enjoy Elysian Plain and I have no issues at all." Joy now filled the returned home vagrant. Theo continued to observe to see if, once he had separated them, the man was going to welcome the woman. He knew Lilith had come with tricks to turn the humans against him, so when he saw that Adam had welcomed Lilith and given her a place in Elysian Plain, he was grieved in his spirit.

In response to Adam's warm greetings, Lilith therefore stated, "I just love this female and you said her name is Eva, right? " Since we are alike, I also enjoy that name. I wish we could help you with your needs and share so much together.

Adam pivoted to face Eva, whose face was fixed downward on the golden surface she occupied. Lilith massaged Adam and Eva's shoulders as if they were making a vow as they drew in closer.

"Let me be driven from this magnificent Elysian Plain and let my soul die until it becomes extinct if I cause any harm to you. Nevertheless, I promise you that I will serve you and do all in my power to protect you for the rest of my life. I am and always will be an eternal existence. I will work with you to produce a greater yield during the harvest season.

I promise to watch out for you day and night, and I will make a vicarious sacrifice to ensure your safety. For you have been spied upon and evil purposes have been planned against you.

Though I am capable of handling your opponent—the same person who is actually Theo's enemy—I will mediate any disputes that may develop between you two.

I'll see to it that you lead a peaceful, harmonious life and that your privacy is respected. I will help you finish any assignment that Theo gives you if I lend a helping hand.

I need a second chance, Adam, my husband and king. Please pardon me for all of my transgressions and let my love for Eva to be demonstrated every day." She promised.

Therefore, Adam replied, "So be it, I give you my consent to do what you want to do according to your vows from this day on." As you have been commanded to do since your creation, teach Eva everything she needs to know. Ensure that there is harmony and serenity among the three of us.

Please understand that my affections for you have been shut off and that my love for you has been fully transferred to Eva." Lilith chuckled a little because she was aware that emotions just don't go away.

She retorted, "You are a man and you don't have any proof of that. I can't wait to swoon over you and try to get you to change your gender to that of a man. Though I respect and love your wife, Eva, and Theo is aware that you still have feelings for me, the sentiments just don't go away. I refuse to gaze upon you in a way that would cause you to forget about Eva and develop feelings for me. I'll teach her what it takes to be a successful lady and how to keep your relationship going strong."

Adam felt compelled to respond. "Theo has already taught her everything and she knew her mandate from the day of her creation," he remarked as a result. Lilith saw that a lot of information was still hidden from them, though.

She replied, "Not everything, in response, as you haven't touched the tree of knowledge of good and evil, which would elevate you to the status of gods with knowledge of both good and evil. As a result, until you eat and benefit from the fruit of the tree of the knowledge of good and evil that is put close to you, you will not yet possess wisdom." The man was shocked, wondering how Lilith came to know this information when Theo had never said anything to him.

"How did you know about the tree since Theo didn't tell us about it," he inquired. Then he asked Lilith to clarify. She could see that she and Adam had a strong bond now. Even with Eva present, who appeared to be a newborn fresh out of her mother's womb.

Lilith answered, "He knew you would see it on your own or that I would tell you so you could eat it and feel like a man. I was endowed with wisdom upon creation to help you see, so that you might not remain forever in the dark.

I was created to fulfill your desires with love and to take you to places you've never dreamed of. I was meant to assist you, just as Eva will, and I can see things ahead of time, but something is still lacking. You must acquire wisdom and understanding about good and evil in order to understand the purpose of life.

You could believe I'm jealous of your wife, but I want to share with her the knowledge I was endowed with at the time of my creation. Regretfully, I am not Theo. Adam answered, "Let us consult Theo and he will be the one to teach us," afraid to go against the advice Theo had given him. The woman accepted the man's request without any problems. She retorted, "So be it, Adam, and trust me or not, he won't tell you the truth about it because he might think that you will rebel against him."

He will believe that you would act in the same manner as Phosphorous, who gave him charge of his angels. However, I have come to humble myself and beg for a second opportunity to live on Elysian Plain among you and Eva." After being expelled, she gained a place in her home by her humility. Though Theo had exiled her, it appeared that he did not approve of her being close to his children. Lilith then embraced Adam and Eva, but they just kept staring at one another silently.

8

Lilith beguiles Eva

Eva grinned as she looked down, then raised her head to see Adam, who was oddly staring at Lilith. He turned to face Eva and smiled at her, and Lilith returned the smile. He had seen that Eva was staring at him. They just embraced the silence as they stood there without saying anything. Lilith was so anxious that she left Adam and Eva holding hands and took a step back when the dark cloud that had been before her obscured them.

The dark cloud split them apart as they wondered what was going on.

The dark cloud carried Adam and Eva toward the center of the garden, leaving Lilith alone. They were to learn about the tree of knowledge about good and evil from this.

Furthermore, Lilith was stuck in the area by the dark cloud, which made it very difficult for her to move. As Adam and Eva reached the forbidden tree, Theo communicated via the cloud.

"Humans, this is the forbidden tree, but it contains evil, and the day you eat of it without my permission, you will die," he declared. "Lilith has opened your eyes to tempt me, but I kept it hidden from you because I knew you would be corrupted by its flavor and starve to death.

You have chosen to allow her to reside on Elysian Plain as a king. You own her, and I don't mind at all, but if you decide to disobey my heavenly directives, I will undoubtedly kick you out of my presence. Before deciding to come back to you, you will be discovered to be as hungry as Lilith was, and I will cover my face." Adam shook and said, "She made a vow to preserve us not disturb us as a perpetrator and lead us into temptation because she is one of us as a humankind," realizing that his father was unhappy with his choice to let Lilith reside in Elysian Plain. "She hasn't gotten what she wanted and that is why she has brought herself to you as a humble female only to beguile you so that you may revolt against me," Theo remarked in response to Adam's explanation. "You seem to adore her and desire to marry them both, but use caution." He added.

Adam honored his promise to let Lilith reside in Elysian Plain. He continued to speak up to protect Lilith from being taken away from him by Theo once more. It's true that despite getting a new wife, he still had feelings for her. "She has no one by herself and her friend Phosphorous, who has been trapped in hell now, she is alone," he retorted.

Thus, his conversation demonstrated to Theo his love for her. "You let her to take you from Eva, my priceless hope for the foundation of the future generations of Midgard," Theo then stated. Adam and Eva were holding each other tightly as they talked, appearing afraid as they stared up at the pitch-black cloud that was erupting in flames and shooting sparks.

Adam responded, "No, I didn't, no one will separate me from Eva, she is the flesh of my flesh and the bone of my bone," to Theo's leaked talk. She is a lady because of this since I and her are one people." After laughing at this, Theo remarked, "I know, peace be unto you man of polygamy."

"She is not my wife, but rather my friend, and she loves Eva and me and promised to protect us," Adam retorted. Theo was well aware that Adam would not thwart Lilith's ambitions because it is her goal to become independent. "It's good to talk, hard to do, but please don't let her trick Eva into eating from the forbidden fruit tree and getting corrupted—she will definitely die," he said. When Theo spoke death, Adam didn't get what he meant. Thus, he enquired, "What is death anyway, and how should she die?"

Theo said. "But right now, I won't waste my time explaining death, which has not yet arrived."

They were returned to Lilith by the dark cloud. They discovered her sound asleep. She awoke from her lying position and took a seat when she felt their presence. Eva asked Lilith about death while sitting next to her on the left and Adam on the right.

Eva had never spoken to Lilith before since her creation, until now. "Mrs. Lilith, what is death? Your father told us it hasn't happened yet, but what does that mean? As a result, it will only be experienced by us as humans. He is unable to go into detail about what we might encounter in the future, should it materialize."

Lilith clarified, saying, "It's the end of life and the loss of Theo's spirit, presence, and influence from any creation.

Your body ceases to function because your soul has separated from it.

You are like a rock that never moves and continues to seem as though nothing happened when you are dead. It can be thrown anywhere by anyone or anything.

Since the soul is what keeps everything alive, feelings diminish and senses disappear with death. Nothing is audible, visible, tasted, or felt by you. Until you are reduced to a skeleton, your body either rots away or is devoured by scavenging animals or avian birds.

Your body's structure is made up of these bones. When anything dies, its original components will dissolve and become corrupted.

When people pass away, their bodies eventually dissolve into dirt and water and their spirits depart."

Adam interjected, "Theo might never do such a thing as leave us to be corpses and let our bodies return to dust just because we ate from the tree he planted and set in front of us," "he forbidden tree bears fruit, however this tree does not wither throughout the dry season." He added.

Lilith spoke, "It seems to me that before giving it to you as food, he wants to see if you can keep his commandments. He told you not to let me beguile you." "Though he is preparing you for Midgard's life, he wants to demonstrate your love and patience. Which would you prefer—eating and growing wiser, or waiting a lifetime for a promise that would never come true?"

Eva stated, "It is better to wait and know that you will reap its benefits eventually than to wish for something you will never have." "The tree has a good taste and can be eaten."

Lilith answered, "Let's see what he does; let's wait a little longer."Because of His immense love for us, God never tempts us by placing the tree of knowledge of good and evil in front of our eyes. This tree will provide a signal for you to consume. After Theo forbids us from eating from it for a bit, we will celebrate and give thanks for his affection. His will for you is that you bear fruit, multiply, and replenish Midgard. He will thus permit you to eat at the time he has set." Eva stood up and faced Lilith, who had taken a seat, demonstrating her enthusiasm.

Then she continued, "I'm excited to experience what it's like to be able to distinguish between good and evil, to have a discerning spirit that allows one to separate the two."

Lilith answered, "It's only that you know that you have a vagina and Adam has a penis that you can place in your vagina to have sex and get pregnant. I'm eager to introduce the upcoming Midgard generations. It's realizing that in order to really appreciate life and fall in love, Adam should have sex with you."

Theo was observing Eva in the meantime, fascinated by Lilith's conversation and feeling like he could be a part of all she was describing. They laugh as if there has never been conflict on the Elysian Plain while they play more and Eva chases Adam. Not touching the tree of knowledge of good and evil, they rose and stood before it.

A number of animals chased after one another and ascended the trees as part of the activity.

Lilith would be beside them giggling as Adam and Eva climbed up to ride the horses and giraffes. Feeling happy that they were enjoying themselves, Theo watched people and animals in his garden and accepted Lilith into his heart.

They kept playing these games until Theo, who welcomed Adam and Lilith's happiness with all of his heart, cemented their bond. Days went by, and Theo never gave Adam and Eva the go-ahead to eat from the tree. Lilith tried to remind them of it as Eva had already forgotten about it and she wanted them to learn about good and evil just as she did.

She eventually succeeded in getting them to consume the forbidden fruit. She once left Adam to play with the other male animals and went on a walk with

Eva to the forbidden tree, where they stood beside it. Eva was then questioned by Lilith, "How much do you love Adam?"

"I cannot measure my love for him because he is in me and I am in him," Eva retorted. I only work for his honor, and he works for my prosperity.

Lilith remarked, "A woman is the one who initially gives her man permission to express his feelings for her. It's acceptable for the three of us to play, but it would be more enjoyable if we had already planned for our future generations and had engaged in play with kids rather than animals.

We have to engage in sexual activity with our spouse in order to feel that sex sensation."

Then Eva said, "Theo is working on it, and the day will come when we can eat from the tree of the knowledge of good and evil."

Then Lilith stated, "The time is right only when there is a promise for it to happen."

This seems to me to be similar to a prohibited experience that you will never be able to have again. You should put some pressure on Theo to carry out his plan for you. Adam missed me, which is why he created you, but I've never arrived on time. Theo will come and stop you if you take even a single bite out of the tree. You will be able to eat from the tree the next day, his angels will assure you.

If you eat it just once and allow wisdom to teach you what is good and evil, you too will become a goddess, just like me. You can become a maker like Theo with just one bite.

Let your womb bear human offspring in the future, and let us watch as they bear fruit for their own generations and the generations that follow. You only need to sample the fruit from the tree of the knowledge of good and evil once to gain your independence.

You would let Adam to worship you, and you would never live to please him again. My feminism will then permeate you and your descendants, and generations after you will be aware that Lilith was a real person. Because of her affection for Eva as her husband's wife, she gave her advice on how to practice feminism."

Eva lost consciousness while Lilith continued to speak, and she also lost self-control as the spirit persisted in getting her to consume the fruit of the tree. Then, while she was reaching out to get the fruit from the tree, Adam materialized in front of her, perched atop a tree, and observed her doing so.

She then declared to Adam, "She perched on the tree branch and took a nibble. "I have tasted the forbidden fruit and death has not occurred. I have disobeyed Theo's law and breached his commandments. I've used my daring and I've come out on top, no damage done. Prove your love for me and keep your promise to keep Eva a part of you, as I am the real bone of your bones and the flesh of your flesh. Nothing can keep us apart.

You can find out if you will die at all by using the fruit of the tree to acquire wisdom, just like I did. Look, I've eaten. Take it and enjoy it, and together, let's live forever, with Theo's wisdom and Lilith's understanding of good and evil."

9

The fall of humanity

Adam was tempted to take a mouthful during Eva's speech, but he gave in to her pressure and did as she asked. Subsequently, he sampled the fruit off the tree. He ate it.

Then, when they began to watch themselves being eroded away from the Elysian Plain, something strange happened to them both. They appeared to have awoken from a dream.

The two turned to face one other, wondering what had happened since Lilith was nowhere to be seen. They looked to be in the middle of the ocean with no bottom then all of a sudden they started to drop into deep, chilly waters. Until they noticed that they were nude, they felt as though they were submerged in water. At this point, they started to feel cold, and Theo started taking his spirit away from them both in order for them to perish together.

Lilith remained where she was, observing as Adam and Eva came down from a tree, their bodies bare. But Theo's ghost kept her from discovering them, thus she was unable to locate them.

She thus began to realize that she was at fault for Eva and Adam's deaths. She fell to her knees and sobbed since her transgression was to entice Adam and Eva to commit transgressions against Theo. Eva also fell on Adam when he fell on the dry ground in the desert.

That was the wilderness east of Midgard. Undoubtedly, they told themselves, humanity has fallen. They sat holding each other sadly, thinking about what had transpired, then all of a sudden they were hungry. They could not locate anything to eat, though.

They realized that their only chances of surviving were to toil hard and scrounge for food.

They understood that the only way they could stay warm and secure was if they built themselves a shelter.

To satisfy their empty tummies and stave off hunger, they had to hunt and consume the meat of the animals.

They realized they had really trespassed and that they would never be able to live happily ever again on Elysian Plain. Both Lilith and they missed each other, but Theo had bound her, preventing her from moving. She appealed to Theo, kneeling in the middle of Elysian Plain, to take another look at Eva and Adam and send her to them so she could suffer and live with them.

Lilith pleaded, "I deserve a severe punishment because I have sinned." Without a doubt, I have tricked my friends and driven them from a happy existence into agony and death. Permit me to go along and assist them. In Midgard, they are going hungry. Permit me to assist them when they start to encounter Midgard's hardships.

Allow me to intervene and save them before the untamed creatures of Midgard take advantage of them.

They will continue to experience Midgard's weather all year long, but they are cold and naked, so let me clothe them with warmth. My father, bend your head and show compassion to your creation."

Theo answered before materializing as a cloud behind Lilith, "I have warned them of you and I have seen your ambition and your pride," . My plan has now failed. In order to reconstruct a comprehensive plan and purpose for humanity, I must begin from zero.

You have destroyed all of my possessions and dashed my hopes for my work. Lilith, what were you thinking!?"

Lilith fell to her knees in front of Theo, praying for her life with tears in her eyes and shaky voice. "It has happened, I can't change it, but you can retrieve them if you want to, but please allow me to serve them," she went on.

Theo retorted, "I can't get them back to Elysian Plain, but I will definitely

kick you out of my garden and let you become the lost traveler you used to be."
For the sake of my love, though, I will allow you to meet them—but only in
dreams or visions, as you will remain invisible to them."

Lilith enquired, "How will they know that I am the one helping them through
a night dream or in a vision?" Why don't you dispatch me to personally meet
them in the dense woodland east of Midgard?"

In response, Theo said, "I have broken my relationship with them, but I
shall see you again in the future. So you are going to be my envoy to them. Just
as you showed them the forbidden tree of knowledge of good and evil, so too
will you teach them how to live and how to do things." Lilith now felt hopeful
because of the promise, which demonstrated Theo's kindness to her. "That
sounds fair, but where am I going to live?" she enquired.

Theo answered, "You are a vagrant who has nowhere to settle," after that.
As promised, I shall drive you from Elysian Plain and subject you to their kind
of suffering."

After conversing with Lilith, Theo departed, and she discovered herself
outside of Elysian Plains, beside Eva and Adam.

When Adam turned to face Nirvana, he saw a vision of a human being dressed
in white, with an unclear face, killing and flaying a sheep. He then removed the
skin and divided the flesh into pieces to create meat. After that, he collected
the sticks from the dead, fallen trees and got them ready for the fire. He took
two stones and gave them a stroking motion till sparks of fire emerged.

After lighting a fire beneath the dry wood and grass, he cooked the flayed
pork chunks on the grill. When the image finally faded, Adam was fully
informed. He pulled himself from Eva's embrace and discovered a jagged
stone that appeared to be a sword.

Eva provided him with everything he needed as he killed one of the sheep
that were feeding nearby and carried out the exact action he had seen in a
vision. After the meat was done, they took a seat to eat. After that, he prepared
the sheepskin for covering himself and his spouse by drying it in the sun. They
consequently wore them as skirts. Adam saw Lilith in his dream, but she
seemed to him like a masculine angel, and the memory of Lilith had vanished
from his soul.

When a dark cloud arose, Adam and his wife were sitting by the wood fire he had made for them. They were happy because they thought Theo was coming to visit. Even though they were in a state of worship, the entire sky was covered in a gloomy cloud. They were still on their knees, their nude bodies covered in sheepskin as darkness descended upon them.

They heard lightning and thunder and waited for Theo. As they waited for Theo's voice, raindrops began to fall. They fled and took cover beneath the tree when they opened their eyes to see that it was raining, hailing, and that they were being hit by a whirlwind.

However, a lot of rain fell on them as they fled through the jungle till they became lost.

They sought shelter behind the large tree from a hailstorm that was threatening to cause them harm. They felt the weight of the cold and the rain, but the hail could not hurt them. Eva had a vision of Lilith heading directly from where they were hiding to a nearby cave as they sat down beneath the tree with Eva in Adam's arms.

Eva then got up, pulled her husband, and followed Lilith's directions to take him to a cave. Adam didn't question why; instead, he followed his wife into a cave where they sat in the dark while the floor was covered in sheep's fur and the leaves of fig trees. Adam realized he needed to find a way to produce heat and light, but the fire he had built was extinguished and everything was covered in water.

Thus, his spouse gave him words of encouragement, stating, "This is the life we were meant to live, even though Elysian Plain was just a nightdream." After so much suffering, are we finally being punished? Is a sinner truly being condemned in this way?"

Adam retorted, "My wife, it's over now. Theo is no longer with us, so we need to locate a place to stay and make our own plans for surviving."

10

Lilith strikes Adam with wet dreams

Eva got up and stripped off the sheepskin covering her lower body. Seducing Adam, she fawned before him while standing nude in front of him. Inspired by temptation, Adam removed the sheepskin covering his nudity. Eva fell to the ground on his pelt as he drew her in closer. Yeah, she did. Adam felt his body parts move when she extended her legs and revealed her intimate regions. In order to satisfy her and feel the heat of each other's bodies, he flirted with the woman, and the two had brief sex as Lilith had described.

As night fell, they transformed it into a passionate evening, engaging in sexual activity until dawn; nonetheless, Adam was not the reason behind Eva's failure to conceive.

Despite the intense rain that disturbed them and made it hard for them to hope for the better life they had grown accustomed to, and despite the darkness of the cave in which they slept.

Romantic love characterized the existence of the Elysian Plain and humanity's first night in Midgard. As it turned out, they were meant to awaken in the morning and go explore Midgard and its harsh way of life.

Eva was unable to wake Adam from his profound slumber and instead chose to sleep in his arms. Lilith kept watch over them during the entire night and witnessed their sex acts. She was invisible to them and only showed up in night dreams and visions, thus she was unable to have intercourse with him.

She thus sought to find a way to have sex with him in a dream because she was so infatuated with him and wanted to experience that passionate love.

In his dream, she showed up taking a bath under the waterfall. But in a dream, Adam saw himself giving her a massage while she stood beneath the waterfall. In a dream, he turned sensual. When the sexual interaction began, Lilith was massaging Adam's sensual manhood with her ass. After that, Adam ejaculated, Lilith vanished, and Adam got moist.

Later, when he awoke from his slumber, he discovered that Eva was lying next to him while he was dreaming. Lilith was disappointed because she did not feel the passionate love she so desperately wanted. She used to love Eva, but her jealousy made her envious of her.

She then intended to keep hitting Adam with wet dream so that he wouldn't have children.

Using the fur he had slept on beneath the sheepskin, he cleaned himself when he awakened.

After having a dream about what had transpired, he sat close to his wife but felt no lust for her. When she awoke and realized her husband was keeping an eye on her, she sat beside him in her undies as daybreak arrived.

"When we can take refuge and build a shelter for ourselves, let's try to find a way to a better and safer place," she said, putting her arms around him.

Adam retorted, "We should bathe first so that we can be fresh and have our strength return to us again."

"All right, let's get started. I want to also get my hair ready," Eva replied.

After emerging from a cave, they went to the river to take turns bathing each other. Adam was attempting to convey to Eva the love he had shown Lilith in a dream. Eva fawned and pressed her body against his while he massaged her, but nothing happened. Lilith had captured Adam's entire sexual desire for Eva in order to stop them from engaging in sexual intercourse.

They parted ways and carried on with their bathing. After taking a bath, they changed into their sheepskin skirts and set off to explore Midgard. They came onto an area dotted with fruit trees, where they collected fruit and feasted beneath the trees till dusk.

They saw other apes, including bonobos and chimpanzees, who resembled them sitting outside of their caves as they made their way back to the cave. They made the decision to become friends with them. Instead of consuming this material, the apes went inside their cave and shut it.

As a result, humanity continued on its way back to the cave to rest while carrying the crop of fruits on their heads. During the night, Adam had a wet dream about Lilith. As a result, he cleaned himself with the fur beneath the sheep's pelt when he woke up in the middle of the night, as he was damp. This was Lilith's second attempt at hitting him with a wet dream.

He slept for a few more hours before waking up in the morning. Eva attempted to entice him to have sex because he hadn't touched her since the previous evening, but he didn't react because his feelings hadn't awakened.

Eva began to cry since she was upset and didn't know what had happened to her husband. In an attempt to comfort her, Adam related to her his experiences with wet dreams.

"I had a dream yesterday morning that I had sex with Lilith, and when I woke up, I was wet and lost interest in having sex with you," he stated. I had the same dream tonight, became wet when I woke up, and I still can't get lustful for you. There's a problem."

Eva shot back, "But Lilith promised to look after us and keep us happy," in a furious tone. "Why is she stealing our joy right now? Perhaps she feels envious that I took you away from her, even though I was aware of her scheme to steal you from me. She is no longer a part of us because you are mine and I am yours; even if she tries to come, I will drive her away. Disgrace to her. My spouse cannot be taken from me by anyone.

I'll speak with Theo so he can either recall us or his vision of bringing more of our generation into Midgard. But in order to make our happiness bitter, I will confront Lilith and fight her for the wrongdoing and evil she performed on you." When his wife said that she wanted to challenge the invisible Lilith, Adam assumed that she was experiencing hallucinations.

He retorted, "It seems easy to express my love, but it's hard to find an invisible person. Although I would be happy to support you, I'm not sure how you plan to battle the spirit of Lilith.

Then declared Eva saying, "I will attack her with taunts and she will feel offended and then I will call myself a conqueror.My word is stronger than anything."

She stormed out of the cave, furious because she was unable to see Lilith. She is invisible to them, which explains why. She went up the mountain to fight Lilith, another invisible female creation. Her spouse came behind her, humming praises without using words, and Theo was moved by Eva's complaint about Lilith.

Once they reached the summit of the mountain, she began to curse at Lilith while walking about patting her chest.

she exclaimed, "I am a woman and the wife of the man that you disturb in the dreams every day and night. Your immoral actions disgust me, and your jealousy makes me stand up to confront you as a woman to a woman. Dare you take Adam away from me? You expected me to just sit here and do nothing? Indeed, you have deceived us, and we have never fully comprehended the enormity of the forbidden fruit we consumed, leading to our spiritual demise, and now suffering is harming us.

The reason you believe yourself to be a goddess is your rebellious arrogance.

It seems that, similar to us, you have also received a warning. Though for some reason Theo has kept you invisible to us, I can feel your presence in Midgard.

You are a puckish harlot who is lusting for my husband to prevent us from ever having children, which has made my husband lose interest in me. I can wattle for him to exercise his manhood, but he never gets lustful or erotic for my exposed body, which is his.

This is as a result of you seducing him in a dream and having magical sex with him in the hopes that he will become your husband. You are misguided, and I am the only one—his wife—who can provide him with offspring and generations of Midgard rather than you, Lilith, a nomadic wanderer.

You should come see me so that I may fight you and prove to you how strong I am—I've warned you to stay away from my husband! Please don't bother us if we start to enjoy ourselves. You are an immodest and roving vagrant; never associate with Adam ever again. Get lost and quit tampering with us."

Adam made an effort to calm Eva down and stop her from blaspheming with regard to unseen Lilith.

"My wife, I understand you're upset and have lost hope, but I see this as chasing the shadows and questioning the invisible creation," he added. You don't know where she is. Making the generations of Midgard a reality is both Theo's desire and his duty. He would find a means to get us back together and rekindle our passionate love.

Let's find something to do for fun for the time being, and I'll make sure you're entertained even if I have to use a cucumber or my fingers to give you the desired sex sensation."

Adam continued to say, "I know sex feels good and I desire it too, but if I don't get erotic then there is nothing else I can do," as Eva grinned.

Eva retorted, "I forbear and follow your instructions as a submissive wife, but it's hard to be sweet and laid back when we're going through hardship. Let's figure out a way to stay warm, even if it means caulking the cave and erecting a wattle and daub hut atop this mountain.

This is with the intention of luring a vagrant who is on the run to reside there. Additionally, we must knit blankets and garments out of the fur of these sheep or any other animal pelt.

This will guarantee that we never experience the chill of this transient world of Midgard. Since we are here to stay, we should locate a suitable place to sleep during these terrifying nights in this wilderness."

Once Eva had concluded her speech, a horde of bonobos and chimpanzees materialized, brandishing their sticks as if they were getting ready for a fight. Since they seemed appropriate and fresh, Adam asked them to help him cut the sticks in the trees using sign language.

They began by using sharp stones to chop down the trees and readying the mud to be daubed on the hut they would build.

Eva contributed her time and apes to help build the hut using wattle and daub. However, they abandoned it halfway through because of the darkness that descended, making it practically impossible for humans to see.

As a result, Adam and Eva went back to the cave, but their other aids trailed behind and made camp outside the cave.

11

Lilith finds love

Theo heard Eva's cry as she berated Lilith for constantly hitting Adam at night with wet dreams. His dream about Midgard came back to him as he respected and looked upon humanity. To seek advice regarding Lilith and Eva, he contacted Michael.

"Lilith's position of being alone as a traveling vagrant bothers me," he remarked, expressing sympathy for her. "For her sake, I interconnect you with her so she can leave Adam and his wife alone. As you are free to approach Lilith, the female, and become her spouse, I hereby grant you my permission. Take this action to enable you to engage in the sexual activity she desires, which will result in the creation of goddesses and deities who will assist in serving humanity."

Michael retorted, "Oh my lord, at your convenience, I will take the female as my wife. Do you not believe that other angels will take their own human brides, just as I did?"

Then Theo declared, "Even if they do, it is their free will if they choose to do so, but they will always be part of humanity and never sit at my table without my permission. Humans do not honor my promise, which makes them evil, dirty, but challenging to turn away from.

They will contaminate themselves with Midgard's women, to whom Adam and Eva will be born, and I will turn them away from me. Thus, in the service of my dreams for humanity, I send you to deflect Lilith's attention from people.

I implore you to wed the woman and come back to me when you are ready. You remain my obedient angel and my trusted confidante in whom I place my faith."

Michael left Theo's presence carrying a gold present for Lilith. He discovered her aimlessly pacing the domain, observing Adam and pelting him with dewy visions while she attempted to conceive. As she was plotting a counterattack against Eva's rebukes and blasphemies, he materialized behind her. And, behind closed eyes, she was planning how to hurt Adam even more.

In a soothing voice, Michael said, "I salute you Lilith with a gift. Peace be unto you, beloved child of Theo."

Lilith scolded the angel, stating, "I have decided to break the pact I made with you Phosphorous, because you are now a devil," after turning to face her back and spotting an angel that appeared to be Phosphorous. "Would you consider pretending to be Theo's servant today, just to trick me and make me become as terrible as you? Please leave me alone; I have nothing to do with you. What do you want?"

Michael retorted, "I am Michael, not Phosphorous, who is now a Devil." He was bound with chains of the Lord because of my victory. I took him before Theo, who banished him because of his disloyalty and disobedience in the lord's presence. Nevertheless, I will return to Theo's presence where I came from and continue to embrace his love, which I came to offer to you, if you do not extend a cordial welcome to me as your visitor in Midgard."

As Lilith stepped forward to meet and greet Michael, she shuddered. She approached him, stood in front of him, bowing politely and gazing down at him.

"I salute and welcome you as my new best friend as a lonely wanderer," she uttered.

"You are correct; as I attempt to interact with humanity in Midgard, I am bewildered by what I don't grasp."

With a smile, Michael gave her the gold gift he had brought for her and then embraced her, kissing her once. Though Michael consoled Lilith with words of hope, Lilith felt the warmth of an angel and clung to him.

Then said Michael, "I have come down to take you as my wife and to give you the children you lust after. I will be ecstatic to be the father of your gods and goddesses."

Declared the man who was speaking more over, "without a doubt, they will be the gods and goddesses who will take care of your beloved Adam, your envious Eva, and their inevitable future descendants.

Crying in Michael's arms, Lilith's heart was filled with delight and fear simultaneously. He raised her and set her at his back after that.

They circled about in Midgard's east to entertain her. She did this in order to shift her emphasis from Adam and Eva to him as her new husband. They circled about till she was enjoying the ride and felt happy.

Then, with the help of their companions, they walked to the hut's shelter, which Adam and Eva had chosen to abandon due to exhaustion. They knitted lovely blankets and skirts and chopped sheep's fur, all while working quickly to repair and reconstruct it until it was complete.

After finishing the construction of the hut, they set up the blankets for Adam and Eva to sleep on. To ensure that the hut wouldn't leak, the cattle and elephant were slain, and their pelts were taken off and put on top of the structure. So that Adam and Eva and the other omnivores could eat for days without going lacking, they next built a fire out of wood and cooked the meat over it.

Then, in order to keep the cabin warm, they constructed a huge fire and positioned it all around it. Then, while sitting inside on the sheepskin blankets, they engaged in passionate kissing. The animals who accompanied Adam and Eva outside the cave also saw the fire. They believed that the hut they had laboriously constructed was on fire.

Adam was awakened by them. Together with his spouse and their friends, he emerged to investigate the situation and discovered a miracle.

They circled it when they got there, but the flames kept them from getting any closer. So they watched through the opening in the wattle-and- daub cottage, the ceiling of which was covered in pelts from cattle and elephants. As they gazed at it, the door's flames went out, allowing them to enter. It was a stunning sight. Adam and his spouse came in and discovered an abundance of deliciously prepared grilled steak, along with knitted blankets and a bed covered in fur.

Eva took a chunk of meat and, without asking, settled herself down on the fur cover that had been made into a bed.

She had a really good dinner. Her husband also grabbed a few pieces and joined his wife at the table, where they savored the meat meal Lilith and Michael had made.

The light of fire filled the mountain. The other carnivores that followed Adam received part of the meat from him, and they did consume it. After that, he went back to his wife's bed to find her naked and dove into her for a passionate kiss.

He became aware that he was once again attracted to his wife when they were making love. After their sexual encounter, Eva talked to her husband while he was dozing off in his arms.

"Lilith heard my criticisms and kept my promise to get rid of you," she remarked. "Do you think we would still be in love if I stopped fighting?"

Adam retorted, "It's related to Theo's dream," but Lilith will keep hitting me with this same wet dream until she finds a new husband or I become hers."Theo should help us by clearing the path and battling Lilith on our behalf."

Eva declared, "The path has already been laid out, and Lilith has her fallen angel husband, Phosphorous. Do you recall the moment she left you? I was made by Theo to be with you. I suppose she chose to make amends with him, or he came to make amends with Lilith. Could it be that Theo made a man to meet her, just to get her to leave us alone? Because of the struggles that women are able to face, Theo respects and values the voice of a woman."

Up until daybreak, the fire raged. Within the same hut, Lilith and Michael were also relishing their moment of passion. Though Lilith and Michael saw everything about Adam and Eva, they were invisible to each other, thus neither Adam nor Eva could see them.

Lilith conceived with Eva. Lilith conceived the god through Michael, and Eva conceived humanity through Adam. Sleeping surrounding the hut, the animals watched after their human friends.

12

The first son of Adam and Eva

As Adam and Eva were able to follow their moral convictions, life in Midgard began to enthrall them. Lilith threw herself into helping the two of them. Eva became aware that she was expecting a child, and Theo helped her understand how she would parent her. Lilith and Michael assisted them in completing the construction of the hut on the first night they were there.

Adam learned to farm and till the soil in order to plant various crops.

Eva helped him occasionally, but she was pregnant and was unable to assist him in other ways. Because Eva also became a burden to Adam, the arduous work became more difficult for him. There was nothing he could do but work hard so his wife could eat and feel safe.

One day, while they sat in the hut, they discussed their unborn child, who would be the firstborn of Midgard's future generations. "I guess Theo's gaze is now upon us since we are about to fulfill his dream about Midgard," Eva said as she began the discussion.

"We have established our own protocols without Theo's consent, and he hasn't shown himself to us once since we broke up," Adam retorted.

Do you not believe that he is still upset with us? Keep in mind that since he has the freedom to do anything and whenever he wants, he ought to be the one to visit us."

"Theo has complete respect for his status and does not associate with anyone, especially not with Lilith's angels or us, the rebellion creation," Eva went on.

Recall that he granted us free will to ensure our autonomy and self-control, but we decided to rebel against him and force him to change his mind about his intentions.

Not because he didn't like what we did, but rather because of this, his love for us was lessened.

Rather, he desired to hold onto his dignity as the Creator God who came into being and formed us in order to maintain his position and authority.

He will take us to his paradise if we can learn to submit to him in humility. "If he is not happy with us, how come we can have kids together?"

Adam retorted, "In his opinion, our productivity is a component of his intentions, or as he would put it, it is his vision for us. We are meant to behave in that way, and regardless of his level of rage towards us, his love still envelops us, and he will never again punish us for it. Now that Lilith is missing, what has happened to her worries me."

Eva stated, "She is the one who made these blankets for us so that we may live a comfortable life and she is the one who finished building our hut." You inquire, "So you ask because she's not giving you wet dreams anymore?"

Adam said, "After you chastised her. "No, my love, but I am asking because I have never had any vision that allows me to prepare things with wisdom."

You must have driven her away, I suppose. Now that we will welcome a child, we have no idea how we are supposed to greet and raise the child in this shocking world of mortality."

Eva questioned, "Do you suppose Lilith is aware of it since we are Theo's children and not her creation? Lilith even attempted to take you away from me, which is why we are in this world of suffering and death. Because of her previous evil and disrespectful acts, it sometimes aches my heart to think about her. I can't approach her, but even if she's invisible to me, she can still communicate with me. Before I'm viewed as being as rebellious as Lilith, I would rather keep quiet and bite my lip."

Although Eva smiled, her waist began to hurt. The unborn child within her begun to move as though he was having fun within his mother's womb. Eva found it incredibly difficult to breathe as a result. Without understanding what to do, she would pant and wheeze, and the pain of childbirth scared her and made her believe that she was going to die physically.

Unsure of what to do, Adam grabbed his wife's hands before turning away once more.

He then exited the hut and and approached his wife once more. She begged him to kneel beside her since she could feel the baby approaching. Snatching Adam's hands, she began to exert pressure till the baby emerged.

They could see he was a boy. After his mother bathed him and put him to bed by the fire in the hut, Adam blessed the boy and called him Kain.

"You are the beginning of my future generations in Midgard, which is part of our multiplication as humans, as Theo had promised me he would have," he said in his opening remarks. "Because my descendants are as numerous as the stars in the sky above, Theo commanded me to bear fruit, multiply, and replenish the world."

You are my strength, so I pushed as hard as I could to start a new existence in this realm of mortality. As the first man in Midgard to rule over everything, alive and nonliving, you are the source of my power.

Everything in Midgard revolves around me, and I need you to exercise my primacy.

You, my son, are the epitome of my dignity's magnificence, and it is through you that I shall triumph in Midgard and establish my kingly and ruling status. You are able to act morally and bear the fruits of righteousness because you are endowed with my righteousness.

I cannot estimate the vastness of Midgard, but you are the first indication of my productivity. I am glad that Theo, my lord, is watching over me and will watch out for you."

He turned to face his wife and noticed her eyes as she stood next to Kain. He then got up to give his wife a blessing. "My love, thank you for the privilege to side with me in bringing about the child," he added as he drew closer to her and took her hand.

"We are three now, which means we have brought more humanity to Midgard. We both possess the power to change the course of events and

Midgard's immoral behavior.

There wouldn't be this child I just named Kain without you, Eva.

We still lead happy lives in spite of the difficulties we have faced. It is now that Theo's promise about us is coming true. This is how our fruitfulness manifests itself. I value the demonstration of your allegiance to both Theo and me.

Then Eva retorted, ""My role in this realm is to give birth."

This is what my life is all about, therefore even if it hurts, I have to do it. Being a woman is not something I choose; it is who I was made to be. As a result, all I'm asking for right now is your consideration for my requirements and some quality time.

It is my responsibility to make my family happy, even under the most trying circumstances. I have to hold my anguish within and continue doing my job. That you are overjoyed with the child I recently gave birth to as Midgard's first creation makes me happy.

Since we bear Theo's image and likeness, we are gods capable of creating and imitating him. I assure you that this is only the beginning and that more kids will arrive.

Then Adam responded with question, "What is the plan behind raising the child? Will you continue to nurse him as he gets older? What about the milk that we also consume from domesticated animals?"

Eva declared, "I'll nurse him until he erupts strong teeth so he can chew the food we are able to eat." As your wife, I am the one you should feed with anything and everything that comes to mind."

When the infant began to cry, Eva took care of him and gave him a nursing while Adam looked on. The infant opened his eyes and began to cry out, as though he had glimpsed something unsettling in Adam, and Adam realized that evil was there in his own home.

Eva asked, "How are we going to handle this baby that is crying the same as me when I was giving birth to him?"

Adam retorted, "Perhaps there is evil in this hut; let us get out of here,"

They emerged from their cover and took a position outdoors.

The infant stopped wailing. However, the infant started crying once more as they went back to the hut. The infant stopped sobbing when they emerged from the hut.

Eva inquired, "does this mean the baby and I have to spend the night outside of our protected hut?"

Then Adam retorted, "No, the baby won't sleep in this strong wind," The strange spirits of the night, who eat everything they come across, will bring his death. Our lack of understanding about parenting a child will leave us open to disaster, so we must pray to Theo to help us heal the child."

Then Eva remarked, "Lilith is no longer showing up; perhaps she could help us get over this situation."

Adam inquired, "What if she is the one attacking the child in response to your reprimand that may have made her feel envious of us?"

"My husband, you are way out of your league now. Why don't you do something to save the child?" Eva shot back.

"Do something like what?" asked Adan. Even after you gave him a kiss, the child is still in tears. Could it be that he's not happy with what you offered him? You should feed the kid, I told you. Your breast milk satisfies his cravings."

Eva answered, "Just find some nice-smelling incense and burn it to drive away the evil spirit that is bothering my child." You can also acquire tree leaves and burn them in order to get that smoke. Perhaps the youngster will fare well.

Then Stated Adam, "I'm sorry to break your heart, my love, but anything that smells will clog a child's chest and make breathing harder for them. He will therefore pass away, leaving us to grieve in solitude with no one to console us. He will stop crying if you simply keep attempting to breastfeed him."

When Eva went back to the hut to nurse the infant after being irate with Adam, she was shocked to see that the youngster wasn't in tears. When Adam heard silence, he went into the hut to nurse the child along his wife, yet the child refused to breastfeed.

After the baby had stopped sobbing, Eva was seen sitting down by Adam while the child was being fed by his mother.

"What actions did you take, my wife, to lessen the baby's cries?' he inquired.

Eva shot back, "I went into the hut and fed him, that's all I did, but he stopped crying."

Adam remarked, "I saw something evil was inside, but it's gone now," that was so incredible." I must figure out a strategy to protect my child from our enemies and other ghosts.

Eva stated, "It's best to start by studying herbs, and I suggest that you start by giving them a sniff." It was unknown to me that Theo had taken away your discerning spirit, which I believed to be still in operation.

I'm just offering you a recommendation as my one and only husband, not to incite your jealousy toward Theo."

In response, Adam said, "I'll look for the incense that I can burn before we go to bed in order to call on Theo's assistance and maintain his presence among us."

"That sounds fair, so you're not worried about the smell that could harm the kid and cause his chest to block?" asked Eva.

"My life, your life, and the child's life are all in Theo's will," Adam murmured.

It's a result of my submission and obedience to Theo, my creator, rather than my own strength."

Eva answered, "You will fail at nothing if you do as you say you will do tomorrow."

With Adam's nod, they settled down to sleep and didn't worry about the child till dawn."

13

The birth of a god

As soon as Michael and Lilith had a sexual encounter, Lilith became pregnant with a supernatural kid. His mother's strength and knowledge would be inherited from his father. This would put him on par with Theo in terms of assisting people in their day-to-day needs. Lilith was driven from Theo's company, nevertheless, so she remained a wanderer. She was in the hut with Eva and her husband when she got pregnant, and they both became pregnant.

She disliked living in the cabin that Adam and Eva had been given.

This demonstrates that the hut fulfilled Theo's desire to reproduce humanity in addition to providing Eva and Adam with a place to live. She and Michael continued to explore the splendor of Midgard on the morning following her overnight stay in the hut.

She made the decision to construct a refuge for herself east of Midgard, in the middle of the Pacific Ocean.

They traveled through the ocean, and Lilith thought it was a place to reside.

She asked Michael to assist her in creating her own underwater home.

She would reside therein with the gods and goddesses she would bear and raise through the ages.

Lilith and Michael had a conversation while they sat side by side beneath the water.

"I am currently pregnant with your child, but I am still homeless because

Theo cursed me and drove me from my home," she declared.

They own Midgard, Adam and Eva. I can't just sit there and watch them make love in front of me because Adam and I used to be married but were divorced over artistic differences. It pleases me to make this ocean my home as I gaze upon it. If Theo doesn't call you to him, I also want to build a shelter where I can give birth and dwell among the gods and goddesses, together with you.

Michael retorted, "For the love of my life, I would do what you wish," But tell me, are you going to keep hitting Adam with wet dreams? I inquire because you mentioned that you were unwilling to see him make love to Eva.

"No, I won't, but I will work to serve him and his posterity," replied Lilith. The truth is, I'm sick and tired of living on the streets. It appears that unlike us, humans are unable to access the sea or to survive beneath the surface. Once more, they worry that they might be ingested by marine creatures, which are blind like humans and only see us in dreams and visions.

Michael retorted, "You are determined to use everything that Theo has given humans as a means of dominance," In spite of this, Adam, as monarch of Midgard, has permission from Theo to possess the ocean. Tell me, do you intend to live there forever with your future generations?"

Lilith responded, "No, I only want the colony site and a place I can name mine because Adam and Eva own Midgard. This denigrates me since, although I was formed with Adam from the dust of the earth, I am now his servant along with his spouse. Although I enjoy helping them, my friendship with humans would be cemented if I could claim a realm of my own."

Michael asked to Lilith, "Do you mean that you would like a world made by Theo for yourself and your offspring?" In response, Lilith made an appeal, "Since you are in support of Theo, I would like to send you to question him about my petition, if that is okay.

"Tell him that Midgard belongs to the humans, and that Lilith is going to give birth to the gods. Please create a realm for her to reside in.

Thus, it has nothing to do with the gods."

Then Michael declared, "I will definitely seek Theo's advice." "How would you respond if he said, "Take a temporary residence in the middle of this ocean while he creates a domain for your rightful abode?"

Then Lilith retorted, "As long as he promises to create a realm for me to make it my habitation, I can wait because I am patient." Independence has always been my only goal." As a result, I would be able to establish rules for my household and have power over my kids, and everyone would be able to respect and believe what I said."

Declared Michael, "I'm going to meet with Theo for advice, and I'll be back soon with Theo's word."

Lilith gave a nod, and Michael left her alone, letting her to sit and gaze at Nirvana. Michael went to Theo's throne before him and fell to his knees.

Theo uttered the answer before Michael could interrogate him with Lilith's plea, "I have heard Lilith's cry, and I see that she is concerned. I am willing to fulfill her wish." The magnitude of hell is about equal to that of Nirvana. Tell her, then, that I will split Hell in two and that Hades, the dark half of Hell, will belong to the devils and demons. The world of the dead is this. I have made Hades my waste disposal, so any who violate my commands and trespass here will be tossed there.

But I will purify the right side of hell, which I will give to Lilith so that she might live among the gods and goddesses, for the sake of good-hearted sons and daughters. The realm will be known as the land of the living, or Abraham's bosom. But when she has Abraham's bosom, I'll break up your relationship.

She'll join in with her generations, and you'll come back to me where you belong.

In response, Michael question, "Father, what about your enemies Phosphorous and his army of demons who are imprisoned in hell?" "Do you not believe that they will make their way to Midgard and plague humanity?" Theo retorted, "That won't happen because Phosphorous is in my possession. That being said, only those who are in Abraham's bosom are able to enter Hades. Lilith must therefore take care to prevent her children from going to Hades, as they will turn into devils and plague humanity with the wisdom of Phosphorous."

After leaving Theo's company, Michael returned to find Lilith where he had left her and informed her of all Theo had said.

"Theo said he would split Hell into two worlds, with you and the gods and goddesses occupying the realm on the right. As a result, stay with me here and procreate, for I will not take you into Abraham's bosom."

He said to Lilith, "Unless you let your sons touch you, I will return to Nirvana to serve next to Theo and you will not get someone to amuse you romantically as I do."

Then with joy, Lilith declared, "All right, I'll stay here and procreate as much as I can until Theo drags me to hell," but why, I ask? Is he granting me torment instead of a paradise akin to Nirvana? Do you not believe that he wants me to be like Phosphorous, the devil?"

In response, Michael said, "He won't do that for the sake of both his and my love for you. Not like Midgard, Hell is as huge as Nirvana and has the capacity to absorb trillions of souls for all of eternity.

As a result, he will split it in two and purify the other half, which he will refer to as the "home of the living," where you will have your entry. The world of immortality is far larger than Midgard."

Lilith inquired, "Will I be able to locate humans now?" In addition will their visions and dreams still include me?"

"Of course nothing would change, and Theo doesn't take what belongs to you, only his," Michael retorted. Similar to how he exiled you, he just took away his glory and left you with your own, leaving you exposed."

The infant inside Lilith's womb began to move as she rose up and turned to face Michael.

When Michael noticed the child approaching the door, Lilith extended her legs, allowing the baby to emerge from her pelvic cavity. Michael caught the child, causing him to cry. After being cleansed by the ocean's waters, Michael gave him the name Bor.

Then Lilith uttered these words: "Now that I have you a son and a god, construct a shelter for me beneath this ocean so that I may dwell here with my child." We are awaiting Theo's arrival in the Promised Land."

Michael started building the underwater shelter and paved it with concrete and stones. Along with installing the concrete and brick roof, he also furnished it with all the comforts of home.

Lilith moved in with Michael and her child, and they made their home there.

Michael bestows Theo's blessings on the child.

"Theo, the first god of the universe, has favor with you and will use you to protect the human race and future generations," Michael stated, addressing his cherished son. "Although you were born beneath the sea, you will ascend the Nirvana mountains and establish your throne above Midgard as the protector of the gods and goddesses.

In Nirvana, there are many creations, but they are yours to tend to, not his to elevate yourself above. It is you who opens your mother's womb and feels its warmth and comfort for the first time. Thus, give consolation to those who follow you and shield the helpless and vulnerable.

Although I am an angel and you are a deity, I have blessed you as your father."

He concluded by bestowing his blessing upon Bor and then handed the kid over to the mother. The pair then lived and procreated in the shelter beneath the ocean to the east of Midgard. Following their marriage, Lilith gave birth to the gods and goddesses, who subsequently inhabited the ocean. Lilith and her children were under Michael's care.

14

Angels Marry goddesses

Lilith declared herself to be the goddess whose seat lies east of Midgard, in the middle of the Pacific Ocean. Michael found her superiority unsettling, though, as it was a sign of her self-exaltation. Since Michael was giving Lilith the self-control she so desperately needed and wasn't manipulating her the way Adam did with Eva, Lilith was able to find independence. Her life continued to revolve around men, but she didn't feel totally at ease.

She extended her progeny eastward of Midgard and had far too many sons and daughters, but she managed to survive under Adam's rules.

As a result, the wives in her generation lived under the supervision and scrutiny of their husbands.

They got married in the same way that Lilith's offspring did.

She conferred with her husband as they sat by the sea, basking in the splendor of Midgard's sun, which warmed rather than scorched their bodies.

"I feel happy and free to see all that you have done for me and Theo," she asked him. "I can now call myself a goddess since you have made me the finest lady in the universe.

Though I am the mother of these enormous beings that I refer to as the gods and goddesses, what is their profession and what part do they play in the universe as a whole?"

Michael retorted, "To protect the offspring of Adam and Eva and to join me as the most knowledgeable and formidable men and women in the fight that the host of Nirvana is expecting."

Lilith inquired, "Who will start the conflict because Theo split us off based on our personalities? There is no guarantee that Theo will ever be able to free Phosphorous from his hellish imprisonment. Despite the fact that hard labor is their daily bread, Adam and Eva are content.

Since we didn't want to be jealous of Adam and Eva and have our offspring battle the human race, you and I decided to own the ocean."

Michael retorted, "My daughters are the goddesses, and they are lustful for the angels who serve before Theo." They are free to descend at any moment and take my kids as their wives.

From then on, Eva bore children whose beauty would attract the attention of angels, who would then descend to take them as husbands. Theo would then become enraged at his creation in its entirety.

The fight between the gods and the devils will be fought by him, and he will set Phosphorous free to discipline all of my children and Adam's offspring."

In daylight, my love is a myth. How could you have anticipated something like this?

Do you really think that people will ever marry angels as enormous as they are, despite how little they are?

What kind of creation are they going to make? Lilith queried.

"The same enormous offspring as yours may shrink down to a tiny size and level due to their disobedience of Theo's orders. A baby develops to be the size of his father and a youngster to be the size of his mother thanks to the light of the sun. A baby's size is determined by its womb fit. Do you really believe that someone as big as me should have such a tiny vagina?" Michael said.

Lilith leaped on him, giggled, and fell back into his chest.

Michael was unable to make out Sepoy and three of his fellow angels, along with Theo's agents of communication, at the top of him.

"What do you want, sons of Theo, and what brought you to Midgard without Theo's consent?" Michael said, standing in front of them as Lilith leaped away.

Sepoy declared, "We are here to take our brides among your offspring. It's our right to do as we choose, you know. So Theo, having heard our petitions, has granted us permission to form a bond with your offspring as well as to take brides for ourselves.

We take these steps to establish a connection that will grow into a partnership, enabling them to understand their origins and stop being barbaric in the long run."

Michael questioned, "Why didn't Theo tell me about this because I wasn't expecting someone to come down and take my children as wives because they marry each other?"

Sepoy answered, "We will not defend Midgard, and Theo will release Phosphorous if you do not trade your children with us then. We'll undoubtedly see it collapse right in front of your eyes.

You are aware of the power of Phosphorous's soldiers, and you also understand that you have no defense if Theo withholds his weapon from you."

Michael inquired, "Why threaten me, Sepoy, and what have I done that makes you and the Nirvanans envious of me?"

Sepoy answered, "You know we feel the same way about you, but you refuse to give us the children we want as wives." We believed Theo intended for us to marry your offspring since he did not provide us with any ladies to accept as spouses."

Michael then stated, "Let me confer with my spouse and the mother of the gods and goddesses so that she may address you regarding her offspring."

Sepoy answered, "Please don't trick us; we are an army five times stronger than your forces, which are made up of your children. You have our consent to do so."

"I have an army of the gods, not angels who are more powerful than me," declared Michael.

"And Sepoy to my gods, who do you think you are? You know what, we are a happy family here in Midgard, and you have no intention of taking my children as your brides. What are you doing when we are also assisting people?"

Sepoy retorted, "We have Theo's consent. If you don't believe us, we may go and consult Theo in Nirvana."

Michael then remarked, "That would be okay, and I would be happy to release my children for you to wife." Only if Theo explicitly states as much, and I can see that he does so by listening to the words that come before his voice."

Michael was boiling in anger and he turned to his wife and said, "Trouble is at the door and peace will be found after the battle.

I am preparing to consult Theo concerning the petition of these men.

They came only to take my children as their wives and they have Theo's consent but I didn't discern this situation."

Lilith said, "Turn to Theo; it was he who sent you to accept me as your wife."

You and Theo have formed an alliance in relation to me. Instead of making threats based on the hope of going to battle, I urge that you stay in peace and come back to me in a spirit of joy and power. I don't want Midgard to resemble the disgusting chaos that Nirvana once was, back when Phosphorous was under Theo's direct control.

She gave her a kiss as they walked off the shore. Then Michael and Sepoy materialized in Nirvana in front of Theo's throne. When Lilith returned, she discovered her offspring, who are led by the firstborn Bor, singing and dancing. All was well, and she went to join them. When they got to Theo, Sepoy and his angel, Michael, knelt before him.

"Father, may I inquire if I am still considered one of your sons?" Michael said.

"You will always be my special son, and I will always be proud of you," Theo retorted. He went on to say, "my son, I don't want you to be upset with me. I gave my approval to your brothers' request to marry your children because I was sick of depriving them of their necessities."

"Are they trying to bring them up to Nirvana?" Michael inquired.

"No, but they will live with you among the gods and become a part of the gods' culture and customs," Theo retorted. Then continued, "but Nirvana is not the home of the gods whose veins are filled with human blood; rather, it is the home of me, the God, and my angels."

In response, Michael retorted, "Midgard will be in chaos, even my children will be like these rebellious angels. They will infuse them with their rebellious spirits, and you will execute them out of rage."

Theo answered, "Don't be afraid; you are an angel sent by me to take a woman as his wife so that Adam will no longer be plagued by the wet dreams Lilith gave him. You are still on my side and will control my host as your myrmidons regardless of any destruction that takes place."

"What about the threats your angels conveyed regarding Phosphorous's release if I refuse to give the angels my goddesses," Michael questioned.

Theo retorted, "I don't threaten my sons, but when destruction strikes, I will release Phosphorous to punish you in the gods' fight against the devils and to demonstrate your sons' strength."

Michael declared with gladness, "The gods are stronger than the angels and are always prepared for war," Is it what you wish, that humanity suffer for all eternity when Phosphorous is released?"

Theo retorted, "Nay, but the gods will vigorously carry out their obligations to protect humans, and the demons should never be allowed to enter the human race."

"I surrender to your will, father, and I will give my children to the angels," declared Michael. "Nevertheless one thing you should be aware of is that Midgard will always be a terrible mess, the entire world will be an area of conflict, and far too many people will die."

Theo retorted, "My son, do not be afraid. You are safe from harm because you are the captain of my host. Please give your brothers what they truly want and release me from their never-ending demands that depict me as a cruel father.

"I will give them father, and I understand that they are demanding their right because of their free will." Michael uttered.

Theo gave a nod, and Michael proceeded to Midgard alongside Sepoy and the angels in need of spouses based on the quantity of goddesses up for grabs.

When they came, all of the goddesses who were unmarried were separated from the goddesses who were married.

Seated next to their spouses on their thrones were all the married gods.

They were sitting in a circle when Michael and his angels appeared among them, putting an end to the festivities.

"Thank you, my children, for this opportunity to introduce my fellow

Nirvanans and the servants of my father, Theo," he said to them. "It doesn't matter that you are unaware of him. The fact that no goddess would be left unmarried is of the utmost importance in this situation. These males I have brought here are interested in marrying and becoming part of the gods' empire.

The single goddesses let out a joyful scream as the round of applause was shared, and Michael kept talking.

"This festival will turn into a marriage ceremony, and all the single women will present themselves to the angels they cherish," the speaker declared.

With their identical regal garments on, the angels formed a line, seemingly forming a single human group.

Every goddess rose to her feet and leaned into her beloved angel. Every goddess clasped hands with the angel of her choosing.

The festivities then carried on, and angels started living beneath the seas of Midgard. Michael walked to his spouse and they danced, with every angel dancing by their respective goddess.

15

The angels Marry women

I t happened in Nirvana, shortly after a few angels moved to Midgard and wed the strongest goddesses, Lilith's offspring, whose duties included protecting humanity. The right to marry the goddesses, which other angels were granted, was claimed by a group of angels who assembled before Theo. This can be attributed to the stunning appearance and intriguing behavior of the daughters of Midgard, who were the offspring of Adam and Eva.

Many of them were virgins to this day. Because the archangels and their guardian were not present, Nirvana was in chaos. With fresh angels to anoint, Theo intended to give them leadership roles and guarding duties. Theo turned to face the angels who were standing in front of him and began to complain. They begged him to give them their rights, so they might marry the women and return to Nirvana.

Theo then asked them, "You know that you can go whenever and wherever you want, so why are you all gathered in front of me?"

Remarked Sinai, one of the angels, as he approached Theo and knelt down, "our protest is not meant to dishonor you, but we would like to know if we could take the children of men as our wives and still return to Nirvana," Although some angels married the children of Lilith, the goddesses, they never made it back to Nirvana.

We have no desire to leave Nirvana, and we have no intention of breaking your decree. Indeed, as long as we heed the wishes of other angels, we are free to behave as we like. We wish to follow the example set by other angels, yet we are scared of forfeiting our rights and duties in Nirvana.

Theo answered, "I am a long-suffering ruler who underwent anguish that no man could possibly undergo. Granting you rights is a means of bestowing upon you the advantages that will enable you to achieve maximum prosperity. I want the most out of whatever you do because I love you. But Nirvana is not a place where gods or humans reside.

In Nirvana, I am the sole God, yet the other gods work with me to perfect my domain.

I will undoubtedly permit you to wed and have human children as spouses.

Regardless, they are unclean, and having intercourse with them will undoubtedly contaminate you with their misdeeds. Since Nirvana is my home and kingdom and I am holy, I would reject you for that reason."

Sinai retorted, "Now that you've spoken, we understand. We apologize for voicing our objections in front of you.

Theo remained silent, so Sinai got up, faced the angels, and uttered the words, "It is allowed to take human daughters in exchange for being married but keep in mind that Theo is holy and does not associate with sin, which destroys human children." You are free to depart, but if you do, please stay in the country of mortality where you will remain mortal and be subject to death instead of going back to Nirvana."

A few angels began to murmur against Sinai. Then, Lakshmi, one of them, questioned, "Who is instructing us what to do or not do, and by whose authority? Who gave you the authority to approach Theo in a leadership capacity?

Michael was able to approach Theo and reason with him after he had taken a lady named Lilith and created the gods. Since Theo is holy, engaging in sexual relations with a man's offspring will count against you as a sin.

Michael, what about him? Given that he had impregnated a vagrant and sex worker from Midgard, is he not also a sinner? It is unacceptable to discriminate against one class while showing contempt for another. All of us are angels, created by one man, Theo."

Sinai declared, "Theo sent Michael to marry the woman in order to create a godrace dedicated to protecting and serving humanity."

Lakshmi stated, "Our purpose for coming here is to beg Theo to grant us human children." We shall also give birth to enormous individuals who will be visible to other humans and assist them in their daily labors."

Stated Sinai, "It is your freedom to depart, Lakshmi, and to take as many women as you like as your wives, but keep in mind that sin will follow you since that is the law. Theo commands that anyone who disobeys them will be executed, and they will shrink to human size and become mortal like children of men.

"Theo is our father," stated Lakshmi. He is the one who tells us what to do and has the ability to speak for himself."

Theo responded, "Go and take the children of men as your wives and return unto me when you want to," in reference to Lakshmi, as Sinai turned and gazed at him. Then Theo added, "Nevertheless, you are immortal angels who will always serve before me, and your offspring will die like all people do."

Without hesitation, Lakshmi left Nirvana alongside his fellow rebellious angels but Sinai and the obedient angel stayed with Theo and rejoiced before him. When midday arrived, Lakshmi and the other angels had taken up residence in Midgard, where the children of men were amazed to find angels dressed in regal regalia and blowing trumpets.

They began the song, to which everyone in the audience joined in, and the show began high above the ground, where everyone could see them. Lakshmi and his entourage of angels sang and danced as the humans halted whatever they were doing.

Eva and Adam lived in the hut they had constructed for the most part during this time because they were quite old. Michael erected this cabin eight centuries ago, and the city now recognizes it as a heritage property. And a city had been established around it by their firstborn, Kain. When they heard the sound of voices and screaming, they managed to get up and went outside to see angels performing.

Upon seeing Adam emerge, Lakshmi descended to greet him, allowing the other angels to carry on with their entertainment. Lakshmi materialized in front of Adam and his wife, who were seated on a wooden chair. They were in excess of eight centuries old.

Lakshmi was surrounded by people who had come to see his discussion with their parents and ancestors. Lakshmi, who was as tall as a tree and had a shimmering physique and a royal attire, didn't mind them and bowed before Adam and Eva.

"We have come from Nirvana, the mighty kingdom of Theo, to be your servants and assist you with your daily strenuous labor," he stated, addressing Adam.

In response, Adam said, "What's your name, son? Sepoy is the angel that we are aware of, and Theo used to send him to me when I was depressed and confused after Lilith left me in the Elysian Plain before I traveled to Midgard."

"My name is Lakshmi, and I am not a messenger; I am one of Theo's servants," Lakshmi stated.

"Since Sepoy was a messenger, you are familiar with him; nevertheless, as of right now, he is married to one of Lilith's children, whose stature is comparable to that of angels."

Adam replied, "Where is Lilith now that she is no longer able to access Nirvana and was exiled from Elysian Plain? Tell me, son: because he was single at the time of her exile, who got her pregnant?"

"She lives under the Pacific Ocean eastward of Midgard and the archangel, Michael is her husband," Lakshmi retorted. "They could therefore see how happy Theo was with the union of his sons with the angels and humans. Despite their plans to conduct a wedding beneath the sea, they never returned to Nirvana."

Then inquired Adam, "So why did you come to Midgard instead of following your brothers and taking yourselves wives among the daughters of Lilith?"

Lakshmi retorted, "We saw your descendants as flawless in beauty as the pure gold of Nirvana. We therefore made the decision to come and take your female children as our wives, as well as to live with you, endure trials, and engage in strenuous labor alongside you."

"My children are not as enormous as you are," Adam remarked. "You are as tall as a mountain when you look at yourself. How could anyone want to wed an elephant to a tiny creation the size of an ant? Get to the point, son of Theo, and stop teasing me. Did you simply in this instance to make us laugh and be entertained, then depart?"

Then responded Lakshmi while still on his knees, "Nay, father, but what I said is what I mean." To ease your workload, we have gold and tools available. Theo has granted us permission to marry and procreate in Midgard."

Adam retorted, "You will have sex with my descendants once you take them as your wives." Do you really believe that the virgins you would choose as wives could accommodate your penis's size?" The crowd around him giggled at his tease.

Then continued to heed the fable that they believed the angel was telling, "I would like to show you my penis, or the woman I would most like to be in love with. In return for gold and gadgets to help you with your everyday labor, please bring me the most beautiful woman to be my wife.

I would show her my intimate parts, and she would take me to her private space to demonstrate her state of virginity. If she thought my penis was a good match for her genital region, she would determine whether or not to take me."

Adam nodded with a smile. Subsequently, Lakshmi was presented with the stunning Saint, a woman whose beauty is referred to an angel. Her name is Saint. She was hesitant to approach the angel, but her companions gave her confidence, and when she approached him, he showed her how much he loved her.

When he gave her the pure gold necklace and additional jewels, she was overjoyed.

Adam stated that "You're the first woman to marry an angel because of your beauty." We want you to have sex with him now and then report back to us on how it went so we can approve our wives to the other angels who are entertaining up there."

When Saint grinned and drew Lakshmi into the private chamber, people wondered how a creature of such immense size could have made its way inside their dwellings.

Lakshmi shrank to the size of a human the instant he walked through the door of a private room. The people present were shocked and intrigued to find out what would occur inside the bedroom.

After teasing and showing off to Lakshmi till he felt amorous and engaged in sexual activity with Saint, the woman became pregnant, Saint clothed herself.

When Lakshmi emerged from the private chamber, he did not transform back into an angel.

Consequently, Saint approached Eva and Adam and declared, "I will accept him as my spouse and I will keep him with me." Compared to the size of his torso, his penis is smaller. He will not go back to Nirvana; instead, he will live among us since my vagina has led him to grow into the size of a man."

Even the people were shocked to hear what Adam had been told. Next, Lakshmi showed up beside Saint in the form of a regular man. Adam then remarked, "I am happy to hear that," referring to Saint. He then addressed Lakshmi, saying, "call all your fellow angels and let them take women as their wives."

Saint and their partner were taken aloft by angels in the air they flew above.

Saint let out a cry, exulted, and enjoyed himself while soaring above the earth.

"I have taken a woman as my wife, now it's your turn to take yours as well," Lakshmi said to his fellow angels as he approached them. Let's descend to the human world, where the virgins are waiting to greet you and provide you with some private pleasures."

"Are you planning to change us into your size once we are married to the children of men?" said one of the angels.

"Yes, your penis might fit nicely in a woman's vagina," Lakshmi retorted. We shall therefore settle here, and Michael, along with his fellow angels and his offspring, the gods, shall come to us and create a powerful government in Midgard." He added.

While some angels were ecstatic and rode down with Lakshmi, others fled back to Nirvana out of fear of becoming a part of human life. After the ladies had sex with the angels, who had been entrusted to them by their parents, the angels shriveled and took on the dimensions of regular people.

As a result, they constructed homes, started families, and got married to their wives. They amused people on a daily basis, and people enjoyed being around them. But Theo ignored them since they turned mortal like humans and lost their ability to fly to Nirvana.

16

Giants' birthing and split

The angels coexisted peacefully with humans, assisting them in all crafts and city construction. This includes cultivation even though the land was arid and could not yield the necessary amount of harvest for sowers, and Eridu, the capital city of the Indus Valley, ruled by Enoch, the son of Kain. The huge humans known as the giants were born after the woman became pregnant by an angelic conceiving.

Their size, which resembled that of the angels before they were shrunk, made them feared by the public.

Still, they were quite beneficial. Later, Lakshmi intended to separate them from humans and their parents for their uniqueness and stature.

This resulted from the fact that people put their labor on them while continuing to make fun of them.

He intended to overthrow Enoch, the son of Kain, the ruler of mankind, and establish his own kingdom. In his royal castle, where his grandfather and father were living and waiting to pass away from old age, Lakshmi gave Enoch advice. Enoch questioned while seated on his throne during the consultation between the two men.

"I heard that you are complaining about the hard labor that humans have forced upon your sons and daughters," he uttered. You had sworn to assist people as soon as you arrived to go through our region. But you never made it clear precisely what kind of service you could provide. Please let me know if I am treating your kids unfairly because of the challenging work.

In response, Lakshmi said, "My children are so enormous that the humans hate them." They give them the impression that they are from outside of Midgard. I am therefore saddened by this and wish to establish a city in one of your territories to the west of Midgard."

Then Enoch question sitting on his throne, "Does that mean the end of our friendship and your service to us?"

"No, but your children are making fun of my children and the children of my brothers," Lakshmi retorted. They have to go hunting, but your kids declined to offer them any praise or payment for it. In this city, my brothers perform as entertainers, but they are not paid. The lack of laws in this land, where it is impossible to control the populace, is what most aggravates me. Everyone follows their own wishes."

"You should urge me to follow particular protocols in order to bring this kingdom into compliance, if needed. Since you and your brothers moved to my country, I have been at your side. You want to take these giants away from us because you took my sisters as your wife and impregnated them to create these giants." Enoch stated.

Then Lakshmi retorted, "We didn't know that we would give birth to giants. We have free will, which Theo granted us, so we can exercise our rights. He neglected to mention, though, that we would lose access to Nirvana if we interacted with people. As a result, I wish to keep my kids apart from people and raise them in a city where they can rule and lead the lives they choose."

Enoch declared, "I have nothing against you and your generations of giants," but I would like to make an agreement that prohibits giants from engaging in combat with humans." It appears to me that giants and humans will engage in combat soon."

Then Lakshmi retorted, "Thanks for taking the time to respond, and I appreciate the opportunity." My kids will establish their own cities tomorrow, but their service to you will never end. Please refrain from starting a conflict just because you believe we will understand you and not take sides."

Enoch remarked, "You speak of war as though it's something that's in your mind," Why frighten me and bring up war at this time? You are aware that your giants are capable of absorbing all of these humans in a single gulp."

Lakshmi retorted, "You should gear up every day and keep your sons well-trained because you can even fight among yourselves without the giants," "Every day is warfare."

"Are you planning to take your wives with you?" inquired Enoch.

"Yes, because we love them and they are the parents of the giants," Lakshmi retorted.

Following his departure from the king's presence, Lakshmi gathered the giants and their belongings and traveled west with them. This was the great multitudes of giants and angels leaving. Without questioning where Lakshmi were leading them, the giants just followed.

Ni mold, Lakshmi's firstborn, approached him from the west, even though he was barefoot.

"Father, the Giants want to know why and where you are taking them," he inquired.

In response, Lakshmi said, "I am transporting them to their country of law and habitation, where they will create their own customs and culture."

Inform them that we intend to construct our city and that, rather than the people who hate us and force their arduous labor onto us, we will live to support one another and hunt for our own food.

Rushing to the front, Ni mold perched on a hill and yelled for attention.

"Giants, offspring of angels whose stature is equivalent to a mountain higher than Eridu's trees, the city where we were born and bred, the kingdom of Indus valley," he uttered.

"We are leaving behind the hardships and effort of people and moving toward a place all our own. We will coexist peacefully and support one another here. While we are constructing our city, we shall spend the night in our tents."

After receiving praise, they carried on traveling until they were far from city of Eridu.

Lakshmi, who flew above the earth and peered down at the giants, gave the orders that caused the angels to soar above the giants who were on the ground.

"My children and the children of my brothers, we have arrived at our destination," he remarked, stopping them as they arrived at the location of their sojourn. "We will camp here as we go and develop our city, making it our permanent residence.

We are no longer bound by the bonds of servitude that Eridu's people imposed upon us. You are welcome to go hunting and consume anything you have created, in my opinion.

I think that you happened to be a product of human control. We are now human beings' children rather than their servants. This location will be known as Nod, and in order to keep others out, we should construct our city here and enclose it.

Giants exclaimed, "Yes! Yes!" The hunters set up their tents and began searching for their wives and kids. While the city of Nod was being built, they made their living by hunting and camping at the same location. People questioned where the giants had disappeared to and what had become of them.

This is because Lakshmi abducted them at night and fled with them, leaving the children of men behind. To meet his king, Kain, the son of Adam and father of Enoch, went inside the palace.

"What have you done that led to the giants leaving our land?" he asked him when they first met. Who is now prepared to assist our kids with their painstaking work and skill?"

In response, Enoch remarked, "This kind of work is what led the giants to break away from the humans. The kids you have have never done anything on their own, and you depended too much on the children of Lakshmi.Thus, in order to change the nation and improve everyone's standard of living, it is now necessary to teach our kids how to fight close combat and equip them for hard labor."

"You didn't even consult with us so that we could make deals with the giants," Kain remarked in anger against his son, Enoch, king of Eridu.

Standing up from his throne he sat on, Enoch responded, "Lakshmi didn't want anything to do with people; he is tired of their flaws and yet makes fun of them. How could you treat someone who supports you in everything you are unable to accomplish with contempt? Your offspring will now have to step outside of their comfort zone and take ownership of their own job, rather than delegate it to others."

Then Kain snapped back, "You sound as though you are happy that the giants are no longer there. They are going to assault this city one day, blow it up, and leave nothing alive. Are you still planning on being content with that?"

Enoch retorted, "No, I won't be happy, but I would die fighting, not standing and doing nothing."

"You seem like a fighter. Do you have any soldiers that would protect this city from the giants' invasion?" Kain questioned.

Enoch replied, "No, I don't, and it's time to arm and train them so they can protect the city. Not just from the massive invasion, but also from our southern-settled brothers' invasion. Due of their disenchantment with the giants and angels our sisters had married."

"When are you starting to train them?" inquired Kain.

"I will call the people and tell them about the giants that have separated themselves from us," Enoch retorted. "I will announce this tomorrow."

After Kain left his son's company, Enoch summoned his commanders to the palace hall.

"Your sons and daughters have made the giants separate themselves from us because they turned them into mockery," he said to them when they arrived. "Now that we are on our own, everything that was previously placed on giants will now fall upon us. The time of tower construction and ground tilling will soon come.

It will soon be time to cut down the trees and start a fire. We will now have to deal with the excavation and mining tasks. We are now in the era of weapon development and enormous animal hunts.

We are left on our own; the giants have left, the angels are no longer with us.

Who declared that you would have to labor like slaves going forward and treat them as such? It's time to start training your sons so they can work to keep the city safe.

It's time to take care of the young ones and quit relying on other people to help us.

Thank you. At this point, you are free to talk to your kids and decide what to do next."

With heavy hearts, they left and went home.

87

17

Lilith demands her habitation

In their thoughts, the descendants of Lilith grew more powerful and expansive. Lilith recognized the need for her own world, a place where she could rejoice with her kids and feel liberated.

She conferred with her spouse. She stepped away from the water and took a seat by the shore. She discovered her kids having fun on the Pacific Ocean beaches with the angels that were circling and amusing them.

Michael approached her and sat down to inquire about her well-being as she was enjoying the festivities on the beach while she was sitting behind a palm tree.

"My love, we've grown so quickly. I don't know if you notice, but I know Theo is really happy right now," Michael remarked.

"If he is genuinely happy to see my descendants, he should keep his word," Lilith retorted.

"What promise now, my love, since the children are happy and the gods are still helping the humans?" inquired Michael.

Lilith answered, "You went to Theo demanding my domain, and you returned stating that Theo will split hell, cleanse the appropriate portion of it, and let me to inherit it with the gods and goddesses. You instructed me to continue giving birth to gods and goddesses while you waited a little bit. Theo has not spoken at all and is still silent. Does he want me to remind him of this?"

"I will return to Theo and serve before him once you are established in your kingdom," declared Michael. "Do you wish for us to part ways and never speak to one another again? All of these angels that you see playing with your kids will not go to Abraham's bosom; instead, they will accompany me back to Nirvana."

Hearing that, Lilith retorted, "I forgot that it would be the end of our love affair. What suggestions for future generations would you make, given that, although having established my posterity, I am still a nomad and would not choose to live here indefinitely?"

"I will visit and consult with Theo on your behalf to fulfill his promise," Michael declared. In a similar vein, both he and I miss each other. I shall cherish the memories until we cross paths again at Elysian Plain, but when I return, it will be our final gathering to celebrate our self-discovery and conclude our adventure through Midgard."

Lilith retorted, "do you believe we'll ever make it back to the Elysian Plain? I would be ecstatic and thank Theo indefinitely."

Michael responded "Yes, since Theo is also missing your fellowship, there is hope that you will return to his paradise. He would be pleased with you now that you had procreated and given birth to the gods. Please begin packing your bags and announce this to the gods and goddesses while I go speak with him."

Lilith sprang to her feet, jumping joyfully, and Michael left, arriving immediately before the throne of Theo.

"Father, I greet you with gladness in my heart and I missed you so much," he said as he bowed before his throne.

Then Theo remarked, "I missed you too, son, but before I could separate you, I wanted you to enjoy every moment of your life with the woman you love."

Michael retorted, "I'm ready to leave the woman and come back to you, father,"

Even if my brothers make every effort to engage us with various forms of amusement, there is nothing particularly wonderful about being a vagrant. The woman is prepared to part ways with me as well because I have assured her that we will cross paths at Elysian Plain."

"You've done well, son. I've already divided hell and purified Abraham's bosom so that she and her offspring can live there," said Theo.

"I will let your bride inherit the earth as her home tomorrow when I unlock the doors of Abraham's bosom. You might approach her and inform her of this. But I shall make the gods and goddesses serve people in ways that have never been seen before.

Lakshmi's separation from humanity, along with that of all his benevolent hosts, is the reason they are suffering."

Michael shot back, saying, "What do you mean your angel has withdrawn himself from the humans? I didn't see that occurring, father. Are there any endeavors you have engaged in that I am unaware of?"

"My hosts were incensed when the angels descended to Midgard to wed Lilith's offspring," Theo stated. "Sinai stood up for me, but Lakshmi persisted and made his way to Midgard. I offered him the option to either go down to the daughters of men or stay in Nirvana and spend all of eternity with me.

He might join them and become mortal just like them if he brought his spouse along. Consequently, he made the decision to go, and as a result, he no longer possesses the radiance of an angel and has decreased in size to human proportions."

Michael remarked, "Maybe he thought you were lying when you said he would be mortal like humans and lose his glory."

Theo answered, "Yeah, my son, I am delighted that you have chosen to return back home to Nirvana, but I am still proud of you. It's time for Lilith to prepare her bags and become a queen in her realm instead of a wanderer, so get down and tell her to do so."

After leaving Theo's company, Michael discovered Lilith and her kids dancing on the sand. After descending, he lifted Lilith and they went off together. And the angels followed him, taking their wives with them when they went.

Due to their inability to fly, the gods and goddesses honored their parents, who were hovering in the air.

"We will move to a new home and area," declared Michael as he soared overhead. "The place where the living dwell and where harmony endures forever. We previously informed you of our ancestry and the Elysian Plain, Theo's utopia.

This location is nearer to the afterlife's paradise. It is the home and location of eternity for the gods. Angels like me, sadly, have to return to Nirvana; however, we shall come to you at a specific period rather than stay with you forever.

However, we will get together and celebrate with Theo, our father, at a later date. I'm hoping you would like to say hello to him in person. You will be brought to Abraham's bosom, which is your home, by your mother Lilith.

You will be revered and respected by people, and Theo will collaborate with you. They will see you while you play next to them in night dreams and other forms of vision, but they won't be able to see you. Let me take you home now that you've packed your things.

They called out to him, made their way to their homes, and got ready.

18

Lilith inhabits Abraham's bosom

Lilith had been waiting for this day for a long time. Finally, the time she has been waiting for has arrived. As a result of Theo fulfilling her wishes, she was able to conceive and raise the gods and goddesses, making them the most formidable beings in Midgard. It's now time to bid her hubby farewell.

Her kids packed everything they owned and awaited their time until their parents gave them instructions on what to do next. Sepoy conferred with Michael on their angelic fates.

He found him sitting on the tall rocks with his firstborn, Bor.

He questioned, "My king, I see that it's time for the relationship between the gods and the angels to end. We don't know Theo, our father, because we came here to take women for ourselves, therefore we're perplexed. We want you to speak to Theo on our behalf so that he can welcome us back to his realm in Nirvana. We'll keep serving you under your wing just as we do now."

Michael retorted, "I will definitely make a request on your behalf to Theo. How do you feel about the gods and angels being scattered?"

Sepoy declared, "We would love to move to the new kingdom with the gods and serve under their wings of regulation. We are not happy at all." Although we enjoyed our time with them, we must acknowledge that new circumstances must arise. The gods should set up their own residence and stop being nomads now."

Michael remarked, "If you say you want to go with them, you can join them and be with your wives forever. Recall that Abraham's bosom is but a transitory place, and that Theo will abolish it and return you and your spouses to the Elysian Plain, your ancestral home."

Sepoy said, "This is truly the good news. What is going to happen to Theo's best friend, Adam."

"Adam is on the mortal side of Midgard, so he will die when his time comes, but his soul shall return to Theo," Michael shot back as he and Sepoy began to float around Bor, Michael's firstborn. "His flesh will decay in the earth and turn back into dust. Keep in mind that Adam and Eva were made of earthly dust, and that dust will be their last form after they pass away."

Lilith approached him and drew him in. Michael then spoke with Lilith after leaving to speak with Sepoy. Sepoy went back to his spouses and kids together with his fellow angels. However, Bor was left in the place where he was.

Lilith inquired, "We are prepared since we know that everything Theo creates is always perfect, so we are eager to get started. How will we establish our new empire and when are we leaving?"

"The minute Theo opens the doors of Abraham's bosom, the chariot of Theo shall come and take you straight to your habitation," Michael assured her.

Lilith asked, "So we are going to ride in chariots to get to our realm? We need to get to our destination because we have been waiting for an extended period of time. When would that be?"

This is because I don't want to be referred to as a vagrant any longer, and our attention is no longer fixed on this location. Rather, I wish to rule my realm as a queen."

After Lilith had concluded her speech, Theo's chariot descended from heaven, surrounded by angels and drawn by white horses. The gods were in complete awe at what they saw in the sky; it appeared as though Theo himself was approaching the gods.

Michael approached the chariot midway before the chariot touch down, allowing the gods to enter. The angel who oversaw the effort was named Sinai. They came to a standstill midair, and Michael went into one of the chariots seated on Sinai to speak with him.

"My brother, Sinai, the servant of the Lord, how is Theo in Nirvana?" he asked as he sat down in the chariot to speak with his fellow angel.

"He is doing well and has sent me to come and take the gods and goddesses to their newly constructed abode," stated Sinai. Midgard is mentioned in the west, and he instructed us to inform Sepoy and his companions that they have to make a decision.

To return to Nirvana and serve Theo, or to travel to Abraham's bosom with their spouses and kids. This is due to Theo's desire to prevent them from losing their autonomy and free will as a result of being duped by both Theo and their females."

Michael said, "I have consulted with them and they prefer to be around their wives and wish to be confined to Abraham's bosom with them. I want to live in all eternity with them even when they relocate to Elysian Plain."

"If they said so, then we will allow them to live with their wives, but you and I must go back to Theo and serve him," answered Sinai.

When Sepoy observed that Michael was having a discussion with other angels, he took off to meet him and took a seat in the chariot beside Sinai. They glanced at him, and he gave them a startled look in return.

"Who told you to come up to us because we were going to come down and take you to the place where you should be?" Michael inquired.

"No one, my captain, but I thought to meet you and let you know how I feel about this relocation," Sepoy retorted.

In response, Sinai asked, "tell us about your thoughts on this relocation,"

Sepoy retorted, admitting that he was overexcited but also concerned about what Theo would do to him. "We don't want to be left as vagrants while we were devoted servants of Theo,"

Then inquired Sinai, "Now, what would you like to do? Are you going to Theo with the gods and your women, or are you choosing to travel there with us?

Sepoy retorted, "But we don't want to lose our fellowship with Theo. We want to stay with our wives and our children."

In response, Sinai shot back, "Have you ever encountered Theo since you left Nirvana for the women, the children of Lilith? Just greet him and wish him well."

In response, Sepoy said, "No, we haven't met him, but we'd like to before we go into Abraham's bosom. How does the realm appear right now? Even if it is utterly absurd, you talk as though you have seen it before."

"I won't tell how it appears until you enter and witness it," Sinai stated, adding that he had never seen it before.

"I am excited to meet Theo and give him a warm hello," Sepoy retorted.

Michael stated, "You can go right now, but don't delay too long because we're leaving shortly. If you do, you'll miss the journey and the kingdom's doors will be closed on you."

With a march, Sepoy called on his fellow angels to go see Theo. While Michael and Sinai landed on the surface beneath the Pacific Ocean, they flew to Nirvana and materialized before Theo's throne.

The gods came in, took comfortable seats, and bided their time until the angels arrived.

Theo addressed Sepoy, saying, "I didn't know whether you were upset with me, which is why you never visited me. You haven't been around since you left me."

Sepoy replied, joyful in his heart, "We apologize for leaving you behind, but the warmth of Lilith's children kept us near." Because of this, we have given birth to the gods. Like our brother Michael, the main issue that worries us is what is going on right now."

"My son, what is going on right now?" Theo inquired.

Sepoy retorted, saying, "We wish to accompany Lilith on her journey as she settles into Abraham's bosom with her generations." We want to live and possess Abraham's bosom with them, but we also want to remain in your kindness and friendship."

"You are welcome to come and visit whenever you like," Theo stated. It is possible to accompany the gods, take care of them, maintain your friendship, and prevent others from severing it."

Sepoy inquired, "You mean we should go with them so we can still enter Nirvana? Father, that is so kind of you. Because of your enormously unusual capacity for love, you are something rare and unmeasured."

Theo retorted, "That is what you want, so go ahead and do as you please since stopping you from achieving your goals would indicate that Theo is an uncaring father who doesn't desire what is best for his kids."

Remarked Sepoy, "We give glory to you, Lord, and thank you for your love and kindness, father. We delight in the land of our neighbors because of your loving heart—the heart of a wonderful parent. You keep doing this, and eventually we will get it. The gods are waiting for us, father, so let's go in peace."

In response, Theo said, "Go in peace, my son, and enjoy yourself whenever they knock you down because I will always be by your side."

After leaving Theo's company, Sepoy discovered the chariot was waiting for them.

"What takes you so long while we told you to hurry because the people want to get to their new home," reprimanded Sinai.

In response, Sepoy said, "Even as we accept Theo's affection, we would like to learn what goes above and beyond what you demand from us. We are free to visit him at Nirvana at any time, which means that we may move on now."

Without responding, the gods and goddesses were transported to Abraham's bosom by Sinai's chariots. The gates to Abraham's Bosom were open when they arrived in a chariot drawn by the white Pegasus.

Michael stated to Lilith before going inside, "Now the journey between us as husbands and wives ends here," I am preparing to meet with Theo and tell him about your safety, as well as how the beauty of the cities mirrors your lovely and ambitious temper, but I am unable to enter with you as I previously stated.

Lilith inquired, "How about the other angels? It appears like they are coming into this city with us, but you say you can't." Michael, you are needed, and I will miss you. I beg you, please don't go."

Michael continued, "I thought we had agreed that I wouldn't enter the city and I have told Theo that I will just drop you and then return to him. Unlike me, these angels are not Theo's right hand; they will reside with you.

It is a pleasure to meet you in Elysian Plain, which is both you and Adam's place of residence and Theo's heaven. Keep in mind that Adam's descendants will visit this city as well. You should prepare yourself by becoming ready for their arrival one by one since the life of Abraham's bosom will raise them from the dead."

Lilith answered, "I wish we could spend some time together in the city because I just love you more than I ever have." Please try your hardest to stop by and see how your kids are doing."

"I will do so, my love, but open your heart and set me free so that I can leave you and until we meet again," Michael uttered.

Lilith bid farewell to her spouse, Michael but she would be left with her children. She declared, "Go, Michael, go my love, and goodbye."

Michael departed her and flew back to Theo, but it was a poignant moment for Lilith as tears began to pour. The city of Abraham's bosom, which was as magnificent as the grandeur of heaven, was approached, and they were ready to get out of the chariot and explore it. A stunning finishing touch was the gold floor surrounding each home with the family names.

"You've arrived at the city of Abraham's bosom, and all the houses bear your names as owners," said Sinai, stopping the chariots. If, on the other hand, your name is not included in any of these homes, you must go back to your residence since you are here by mistake. Go to your locations after getting off of my chariot now."

Lilith shot back, "Some houses are far from us and we don't fly with wings just like you do. Deliver each person to their home's door so that no one remains outside the residence."

With a nod, Sinai moved through the city, bringing the gods and goddesses to their new dwellings in the new realm. After he was done, each person went inside their own home. The angel resided with them and they with their wives. Sinai was pleased to see that the family was doing well despite being in Abraham's bosom.

When he got back to Theo, Michael was already in Nirvana, hanging out with him. Afterwards, he joined the Nirvana family.